VISIONS OF
Heaven & Hell

VISIONS OF
Heaven & Hell

JOHN BUNYAN

Whitaker House

All Scripture quotations are taken from the *King James Version* (KJV) of the Bible.

VISIONS OF HEAVEN AND HELL

ISBN: 0-88368-541-8
Printed in the United States of America
Copyright © 1998 by Whitaker House

Whitaker House
30 Hunt Valley Circle
New Kensington, PA 15068

Library of Congress Cataloging-in-Publication Data

Bunyan, John, 1628–1688.
    Visions of heaven and hell / by John Bunyan.
       p.   cm.
    ISBN 0-88368-541-8 (trade paper)
    1. Heaven—Christianity. 2. Hell—Christianity. I. Title.
BT846.2.B86 1998
236'.24—dc21   98-26070

3 4 5 6 7 8 9 10 11 12 13 / 08 07 06 05 04 03 02 01

CONTENTS

1

The Life of John Bunyan

John Bunyan, a name familiar to every ear, was born in 1628 in the little village of Elstow, England, within a mile of Bedford. To use his own words, he was born "of a low inconsiderable generation," for his father followed the universally despised calling of a tinker (a mender of pots and pans). This occupation seems to have been held in low repute in those days, probably because of the wandering and unprincipled habits of most of the tinker fraternity. But Bunyan's father had a settled place of residence in Elstow and a good reputation among his neighbors.

In addition, he saw to it that John attended school at a time when it was much less common for parents in a humble position to avail themselves of the blessings of education for their children than happily it is now. John learned to read and write although he later said that he "did soon lose that little [that he had] learned."

It is clear, however, from his writings, that his memory must have been tenacious to an extraordinary degree and that the other powers of his mind were healthy and vigorous. It is likely that his assessment of what he remembered from school only reflects Bunyan's judgment that as a consequence of his youthful behavior, he lost all relish for learning. He felt that he had added nothing to his meager stock of knowledge until many precious years had been dissipated by him in evil and unprofitable courses. The reader will find a vivid and faithful narrative of his boyhood activities and the extreme distress he felt as a consequence of them in his spiritual autobiography entitled *Grace Abounding to the Chief of Sinners*.

GOD'S GRACE IN ACTION

During his early life, he made some remarkable escapes from imminent danger. Twice he narrowly escaped drowning, and when he served in the Parliamentary army, a soldier asked to take Bunyan's post. That man was "shot into the head with a musket bullet, and died." Afterwards, Bunyan looked back with a deep feeling of gratitude to a preserving and forbearing God who had not cut him off in his sins but had mingled mercy with judgment. Among those mercies, not the least of which, was his being led while yet a very young man "to light upon a wife" who had been religiously educated. Her example and conversation persuaded the young tinker to go fairly regularly to church and to prefer his own fireside and her company to the alehouse and his drinking companions.

The young couple "came together as poor as poor might be, not having so much household stuff as a dish or spoon betwixt [them] both." His wife did have two books that she brought to their marriage: *The Plain Man's Pathway to Heaven* and *The Practice of Piety*. These books had a significant influence on Bunyan's spiritual development.

Bunyan was young, healthy, and had a trade by which he could always earn a decent livelihood. His wife was frugal, industrious, and good-tempered. What more was needed to light up their cottage with peace and contentment except the presence of true religion in both?

To true piety, however, John was yet a stranger. He had acquired a certain taste for churchgoing and a great respect, as he describes it, for "the high place, priest, clerk, vestment, service, and what else, belonging to the church." His strong and active imagination would often be powerfully excited by circumstances that would have made little impression on the average person's mind. But he was still an utter stranger to real religion.

His devotions were as formal as could well be imagined, and they often failed to keep his conscience quiet even though he felt a certain kind of pleasure in returning to them. His religious notions were exceedingly confused and contradictory. They seemed to have been accompanied by a strong leaning toward mysticism as well as bold speculation.

Sometimes he thought that words were spoken to him from heaven. At other times, he thought that new and mysterious objects were presented to his very senses. He would commit himself to prayer and Bible reading with something of a childlike willingness to be taught. Then, he would abandon his study of the Word to lose himself amid speculations utterly too high for him on the subject of the divine laws.

TIMES OF DESPAIR

Sometimes a gleam of light and hope shot across the darkness of his troubled soul, and he thought he could perceive what it was reasonable and expedient for him to do in order to be at peace with himself and his God. At other seasons, the darkness of despair's deepest midnight seemed to settle down on his soul, and in this fearful mood, he would argue thus insanely: "My state is miserable, miserable if I leave my sins, miserable if I follow them. I can but be damned; and if I must be so, I had as good be damned for many sins as for few." Thus, he says of himself on one occasion:

> I stood in the midst of my play, before all that were present, but yet I told them nothing; but having made this conclusion, I returned desperately to my sport again. And I well remember that presently this kind of despair did so possess my soul that I was persuaded I could never attain to other comfort than what I

10

should get in sin, for heaven was gone already, so that on that I must not think. Wherefore I found within me great desire to take my fill of sin, still studying what sin was yet to be committed that I might taste the sweetness of it lest I should die before I had my desires.

A CHANGED MAN

From this wretched course, he was rescued in an unusual manner. A woman, herself of very bad character, happened one day to scold him for swearing. She told him that he was "the ungodliest fellow that ever she heard in all her life" and fit to corrupt all the youth in the town. The criticism struck him so forcibly that from that hour, he began to discontinue the sin of swearing. He also pledged himself anew to the reading of his Bible. His conduct was so changed that his neighbors began to look on him as quite a reformed character.

Formerly, he had taken great delight in ringing the church bells. With his conscience growing very tender, he began to feel that "such practice was but vain." He abandoned that amusement and also quit dancing, considering it an ensnaring and frivolous recreation. A spirit of legality took possession of him; he began to think that "no man in England could please God better" than he. He did not know the necessity of a deeper, more powerful change of heart and nature than anything he had yet experienced; however, he felt certain misgivings and unrest as to his true condition in the sight of God. Happening to overhear some pious women talking about regeneration, he became at last convinced that his views of religion were very defective—that he "lacked the true tokens of a true godly man."

The women to whom Bunyan was indebted for his new light were members of a small Baptist congregation in Bedford of which John Gifford was pastor. Of this good man, Mr. Ivimey, in his *History of the English Baptists*, said:

> His labors were apparently confined to a narrow circle, but their effects have been very widely extended and will not pass away when time will be no more. We allude to his having baptized and introduced to the church the wicked tinker at Elstow. He was doubtless the honored evangelist who pointed Bunyan to the Wicketgate by instructing him in the knowledge of the Gospel, by turning him from darkness to light, and from the power of Satan unto God. Little did he think such a chosen vessel was sent to his house when he opened his door to admit the poor, the depraved, and the despairing Bunyan.

It is affirming too much to represent Mr. Gifford as having been the means of Bunyan's conversion; but that his conversation and preaching were greatly blessed to the once "wicked tinker of Elstow," we have the best authority for believing.

Bunyan endured great inward agitation of soul not only because of his own consciousness of sin but also because of the destructive talk of some Antinomians (who taught that Christ's forgiveness eliminated the need for laws) into whose company he had fallen. But Bunyan had already studied the Scriptures with great diligence and fervent prayer, and by the blessing of God's Spirit, he gained a resting place for his troubled spirit in the scriptural assurance that "none ever trusted God and was confounded." (See Isaiah 45:17.)

APPOINTED TO PREACH

In 1655, Bunyan, then twenty-seven years of age, was admitted as a member of Mr. Gifford's church. Soon after, the church was deprived of its pastor by death, and the young brother so recently added to their fellowship was, after some trial of his qualifications, called on to undertake the office of occasional preacher or exhorter among them. About this appointment, Bunyan wrote:

> Some of the most able among the saints with us, I say the most able for judgment and holiness of life as they conceived, did perceive that God had counted me worthy to understand something of His will in His holy and blessed Word and had given me utterance in some

measure to express what I saw to others for edification. Therefore they desired me, and that with much earnestness, that I would be willing at some times to take in hand in one of the meetings to speak a word of exhortation unto them; the which, though at the first it did much dash and abash my spirit, yet being still by them desired and entreated, I consented to their request.

When Bunyan first began to preach, people came from all parts to hear him. Such was the visible success of his ministry that before long, "after some solemn prayer and fasting," he was specially set apart by the church for the regular exercise of an itinerant ministry in Bedford and the neighborhood.

When he first began to preach, he dealt chiefly on the terrors of the law. About this aspect of his preaching, he wrote:

This part of my work, I fulfilled with great sense; for I preached what I felt, what I smartingly did feel, even that under which my poor soul did groan and tremble to astonishment. I went myself in chains to preach to them in chains and carried that fire in my own conscience that I persuaded them to be aware of.

As his own spiritual horizon cleared up, his preaching took a better tone. He now labored, "still preaching what he saw and felt," to preach Christ, "the sinner's friend, while sin's eternal foe," and to persuade his hearers to lean entirely on the work and offices of Christ. He made it a leading object in his sermons "to remove those false supports and props on which the world does lean, and by them fall and perish."

A DEDICATED WRITER

He now had a sphere of constant activity and abundant usefulness opened to him. With his characteristic energy, he sought to fill it not only by preaching the Word but also by publishing short religious treatises. His first publication was entitled *Some Gospel Truths Opened according to the Scriptures*. To this treatise, John Burton, Mr. Gifford's successor in the regular ministry of the church at Bedford, prefixed a commendatory letter. Burton wrote:

> Having had experience with many other saints of this man's soundness in the faith, of his godly conversation, and his ability to preach the Gospel, not by human art but by the Spirit of Christ, and that with much success in the conversion of sinners, I say, having had experience of this and judging this book may be profitable to many others as well as to myself, I thought it my duty on this account to bear witness with my brother to the plain and simple and yet glorious truths of our Lord Jesus Christ.

The particular occasion of this treatise seems to have been the opposition that Bunyan experienced in his preaching from some Quakers who told him that he "used conjuration and witchcraft" and that he "preached up an Idol, because he had said that the Son of Mary was in heaven with the same body that was crucified on the cross." Against such accusations and in defense of his views of Scripture concerning the death, Resurrection, Ascension, and mediation of Christ, Bunyan argued with great force as well as plainness of reasoning and with much less sharpness and lack of polish than might have been anticipated from the temper and education of the man and the character of the times in which he wrote.

His language is idiomatic but pure to an extraordinary degree for the first effort in composition by an uneducated man. A reply to Bunyan's pamphlet was published by one Edward Burroughs with the title *The True Faith of the Gospel of Peace Contended For in the Spirit of Meekness*. It was a railing and declamatory production, but Bunyan replied to it, and Burroughs rejoined, after which the controversy ended.

SENTENCED TO PRISON

In 1657, Bunyan was indicted for preaching at Eaton. Nothing came of it, although Dr. Robert Southey, a biographer of Bunyan, labored to prove the existence of an extremely persecuting spirit at that time in the British Commonwealth. A few months after the Restoration, however, a warrant was issued against Bunyan, and he was arrested at Samsell in Bedfordshire and carried before Justice Wingate. When Bunyan refused to abstain from preaching, he was committed to the Bedford jail. At the quarter sessions, his indictment stated:

> John Bunyan of the town of Bedford, laborer, had devilishly and perniciously abstained from coming to church to hear divine service and was a common upholder of several unlawful meetings and conventicles (secret religious meetings not sanctioned by law) to the great disturbance and distraction of the good subjects of this kingdom, contrary to the laws of our sovereign lord the king.

On this ridiculous charge, he was sent back to prison for three months and informed that if at the end of that period he did not submit to go to church and quit preaching, he would be banished from the realm.

A FAITHFUL WIFE

At this period, Bunyan was the father of four young children by his first wife. Mary, his oldest child, had been born blind. A year following his first wife's death, he had married a second wife. Her confinement was approaching. News of his imprisonment and the prospect of his impending banishment so affected her that she prematurely delivered a dead child. Yet in the middle of all this complicated suffering, this noble-minded young woman struggled hard to obtain her husband's deliverance. With simplicity of heart, she traveled to London to petition the House of Lords for her husband's liberation but was directed to apply to the judges at the judicial inquest. She then returned home, and with modesty and "a trembling heart," she put forth her request to the judges in the presence of many magistrates and gentry of the county. Sir Matthew Hale was one of them, but he shook his head and professed his inability to do anything for her husband.

"Will your husband leave off preaching?" asked Judge Twisden. "If he will do so, then send for him."

"My lord," replied the courageous woman, "he dares not leave preaching as long as he can speak."

Sir Matthew listened sadly to her, but Twisden brutally taunted her and said poverty was her cloak.

"Yes," observed she, "and because he is a tinker and a poor man, therefore he is despised and cannot have justice." Elizabeth Bunyan concluded her own account of this interview in these words:

Though I was somewhat timorous at my first entrance into the chamber, yet before I went out, I could not but break forth into tears— not so much because they were so hard-hearted against me and my husband, but to think what a sad account such poor creatures will have to give at the coming of the Lord.

A PRODUCTIVE CONFINEMENT

Bunyan remained in prison twelve years, but occasionally during that period, through the connivance of the jailer, he was allowed to steal out under cover of night. On one occasion, he was even able to pay a visit to the Christians in London. It was during this long imprisonment, while wasting the flower of his age in confinement and with no books except the Bible and Foxe's *Book of Martyrs*, that he penned his immortal work, *The Pilgrim's Progress*, besides many other treatises that have afforded much instruction and comfort to the people of God.

FREED FROM PRISON

During the last year of his imprisonment (1671), he was chosen pastor of the Baptist church in Bedford. He appears to have been allowed to attend the church meetings for the last four years of his imprisonment. Doubtless, his word was considered a sufficient pledge that he would return every evening to prison. At last his release was ordered. It is said that Barlow, Bishop of Lincoln, intervened on Bunyan's behalf. Soon after his release, a new chapel was built at Bedford, where he preached to large audiences during the remainder of his life.

Once every year, he visited London, where he preached with great acceptance, generally at the meetinghouse in Southwark. Also, he used to itinerate extensively in the surrounding counties. It is said that Owen was always among his metropolitan hearers. On being asked by Charles II how a learned man such as he could sit and listen to an illiterate tinker, that great scholar and divine replied, "May it please your majesty, could I possess that tinker's abilities for preaching, I would most gladly relinquish all my learning."

The writer of the first biographical sketch of Bunyan described his personal appearance:

He appeared in countenance to be of a stern and rough temper; but in his conversation, mild and affable, not given to talkativeness or much discourse in company unless some urgent occasion required it; observing never to boast of himself or his parts, but rather seem low in his own eyes and submit himself to the judgment of others; abhorring lying and swearing; being just in all that lay in his power to his word; not seeming to revenge injuries; loving to reconcile differences and make friendships with all. He had a sharp quick eye, accompanied with an excellent discerning of persons, being of good judgment and quick wit. As for his person, he was tall of stature; strong-boned though not stout; somewhat of a ruddy face with sparkling eyes; wearing his hair on his upper lip after the old British fashion; his hair reddish, but in his later days, time had sprinkled it with gray; his nose well set, but not declining or bending;

and his mouth moderate large; his forehead something high; and his habit always plain and modest.

HIS WORK LIVES ON

Little is recorded of the remainder of Bunyan's life. It is not known whether he was again made a sufferer for conscience' sake when the spirit of persecution revived and waxed hot against the people of the Lord in the latter part of Charles's reign. He died in London on the twelfth day of August 1688 of a fever that he had caught by exposure to rain. He was buried in Bunhill Fields, a churchyard in London. His widow survived him four years. The names of a few of his descendants appear in the books of the Baptist church at Bedford, but his last known descendant, Hannah Bunyan, a great-granddaughter, died in 1770 at the age of seventy-six.

In 1692, the year of Elizabeth Bunyan's death, her husband's collected works were published in two folio volumes by Ebenezer Chandler, his successor in the ministry at Bedford, and John Wilson, a fellow minister. These volumes contain about sixty pieces of various degrees of merit. All are richly impregnated with the unction of deep and fervent piety.

(Adapted from the introductory notes of Rev. Thomas Scott in *Bunyan's Whole Allegorical Works*, Glasgow: Fullarton, 1840.)

2

To the Christian Reader

The design of the following treatise is for your spiritual advantage. By displaying the heavenly glory to the eyes of your mind, you may have your affections and desires stirred up to choose heaven as your chiefest treasure. Then, *"where your treasure is, there will your heart be also"* (Matt. 6:21). Perhaps there is as much said to engage your affections as has been written anywhere on this subject. Through the divine blessing, may you be inspired to gain the happiness here described, which may result in your eternal enjoyment of it. It does not indeed pretend to give a graphic description thereof, for *"it doth not yet appear what we shall be"* (1 John 3:2), but it gives such a description of it as the Divine Oracles will warrant. It shows wherein the nature of our happiness does chiefly consist and resolves the most profound and curious questions about it according to the Word of Truth.

Seeing love and desire are the wings of the soul by which it flies toward heaven, I do not doubt but that the devout soul will here find those attractions that will gradually draw it there, for what can more engage our affections than the desire to behold that bright *"eternal excellency"* (Isa. 60:15), who is altogether desirable and whom the church describes as fairer than the children of men. And if He was so in the days of His humiliation, how much more glorious is He on the throne, being crowned with glory and honor as the Apostle to the Hebrews speaks (Heb. 2:7, 9)?

Although *"glorious things are spoken"* of the city of God (Ps. 87:3), which is represented to us as an *"eternal excellency, a joy of many generations"* (Isa. 60:15), yet after the most comprehensive descriptions, we will be forced to acknowledge when we come to heaven what the queen of Sheba did when she saw the glory of Solomon: that the half has not been told (1 Kings 10:7).

However, there is enough to engage our hearts, ravish our affections, and make us cry out with David, *"How amiable are thy tabernacles, O LORD of hosts"* (Ps. 84:1).

But as love and desire carry us after what we perceive to be amiable and lovely, so fear is a passion of the soul, and it flees from and avoids whatever it understands to be evil. This passion works as strongly in some souls as love and desire do in others. To these, the visions of hell may be as useful to frighten them from it as the visions of heaven are to draw others to it. Here you may, as it were, place your ears at the mouth of Tophet (Isa. 30:33) and hear the doleful lamentations of those lost wretches who, through a vain pursuit of sinful pleasure, have brought on themselves eternal miseries. Here you may see how they too soon lament those torments it is too late to help. And these should, to all wise considering persons, be looked on as so many seamarks to warn others to avoid the same destruction.

The author to the Hebrews tells us that Noah, being moved with fear, prepared an ark to save his household (Heb. 11:7). If the fear of the torments of hell, which are here so vividly described, moves any souls to get into the ark, Christ Jesus, and so avoid the *"wrath to come"* (Matt. 3:7), it will be an unspeakable mercy.

Nor let anyone be confused that this is delivered under the likeness of a vision, for as long as the truths herein conveyed are according to the analogy of faith, the dress in which they are put may be very well set aside. I have done herein like the physicians who put their medication in some pleasant vehicle to make it go down easier with their patients. And since the way to heaven has been compared to a dream, why should not the journey's end be as acceptable under the same kind of vision? Why should it not be more acceptable, since the end is preferable to the means and heaven to the way that brings us there? The pilgrim met with many difficulties, but here they are all over. All storms and tempests are hushed in silence and serenity.

Let us stay no longer here then, but mount up with golden wings of faith and love:

> *For, lo, the winter is past, the rain is over and gone; the flowers appear on the earth; the time of the singing of birds is come, and the voice of the turtle is heard in our land.* (Song 2:11–12)

The blessed Bridegroom of our souls calls to us, *"Arise, my love, my fair one, and come away"* (v. 13), which, reader, that you may make haste to do is the desire and prayer of,

Your soul's well-wisher,
John Bunyan.

3

The Introduction

When wicked and unprincipled persons have gone on in a course of sin to the degree that they can scarcely hope for pardon and find that they have reason to fear the just judgment of God for their sins, they begin at first to wish that there were no God to punish them, which they think would be in their best interests. And so, by degrees, they come to persuade themselves that there is no God. Then they determine to find arguments to back their opinion in order to prove what they are willing to believe.

A BAD INFLUENCE

It was with one of this sort of brutes, for they are hardly worthy of the name of men, that I had the unhappiness to be acquainted. He continually repeated to me that there was neither God nor Devil, heaven nor hell, and that those things were only the shrewd inventions of those who were willing to keep the world in dread—just, he said, as we talk of goblins in order to frighten children. It was not without horror and trembling that I first heard this conversation; therefore, I usually left him when he began to talk about these topics. But his speaking of them to me so often at last became effective so that I started to consider what grounds he had for what he said.

From that time on, I found my mind perplexed with so much trouble and darkness that I could hardly bear up under it, for I did not know how to make out to my own satisfaction those truths that before appeared self-evident to me. The thought that there was no God caused me the greatest horror, yet I called into question the truth of His existence. I would not have parted with my hopes of heaven to have been made heir of all the world, yet I questioned whether there really was such a place or state. I began to doubt whether there was any hell, yet at the same time, I thought its flames were flashing in my face. Thus, my mind was distracted with apparent contradictions, and I found myself in a labyrinth of confusion from which I had no clue as to how to extricate myself.

THE PERIL OF FALSE COUNSEL

In this perplexed condition, I went to my false friend to see what comfort he could give. This was like Saul's going to the witch of Endor when God had forsaken him. (See 1 Samuel 28:7–19.) What he said did more to confuse me than to satisfy me. He laughed at my fears, pretended to pity my weakness, and seemed to congratulate himself in the freedom and liberty that he enjoyed. He told me that in the pursuit of what he had to do, he was never disturbed by the frightful murmurs of a future state or of a final judgment.

He believed that nature was the great mistress of the universe; therefore, he followed her dictates. All the care he took was to live here so that when his dust would next be infused, it might be into some delightful species of being. His future, he believed, would in a great measure be owing to the place of his burial. If he were buried in a church or placed in a vault, it was possible that his dust might be turned into spiders, toads, or serpents; therefore, if he could, he planned to be buried in a field or garden so that there his ashes might spring up in carefully designed, delightful flowers.

This arrangement was the most happiness he could contemplate for himself. He would be very well satisfied to find all those qualities and powers he now possessed exerted in the variegated beauties of nature. Further, he affirmed, that for all he knew, in the various metamorphoses of nature, he might, some ages from this time, again inhabit a human body as he believed he had done many ages past.

I then presented the Scriptures to confront this unintelligible plan, but he discredited them as being only the agent by which shrewd men brought about their designs. He said that to prove the reality of a

God by the Scriptures was the same thing as to prove the divine origin of the Scriptures by the existence of a God.

DOUBT BREEDS DESPAIR

With these discourses of his causing me further doubts, I felt so uneasy that my life became a burden to me. I dreaded to be left with the belief of those cursed notions, yet they continually ran in my mind. I wished a thousand times I had never heard them, and yet they were ever before me. Were all my hopes of heaven nothing but a vain illusion? Had I served God for nothing? Or rather, had I fancied a God when there was no such being?

It is impossible to tell the agonies I felt from considering such thoughts as these. With great force, they assaulted me until at last, I was pushed to the utmost edge of desperation. Why should I linger between despair and hope? Is it not better, I asked myself, to put a period to this wretched life and to test the truth of things?

SUICIDE CONSIDERED

On reaching this point, I resolved to destroy myself. In order to carry out the bloody tragedy, I went out one morning to a nearby woods. As I was about to commit the act, I thought I heard a secret whisper, saying:

O Epenetus, do not plunge yourself in everlasting misery to gratify your soul's worst Enemy. That fatal stroke you are about to give seals up your own damnation, for if there is a God, as surely there is, how can you hope for mercy from Him when you so willfully destroy His image?

SAVED BY GOD

From where this secret whisper came, I knew not, but I do believe it was from God. It came with so much power that it made me fling away the instrument with which I had planned to do violence to my own life. It showed me in a moment the wickedness of my intention. The horror of this barbarous action set all my joints trembling so that I could hardly stand. Then the fatal precipice of my planned destruction was presented to me in a frightful view so that I could not but acknowledge my deliverance to be the work of some invisible and spiritual power that came to my rescue so seasonably. Gratitude obliged me to return thanks to Him, so I kneeled down on the ground and said:

O invisible, eternal Power, who, though unseen by man, observes all his actions and who has now prevented me from defacing Your image, I humbly give You my thanks. Yes, O sovereign Being of all beings, I give You thanks that I am still alive. I thank You that I am able to acknowledge there is such a Being. Do not hide Yourself in such thick clouds of darkness from my view, but let the Sun of Glory shine on me and chase away the blackness of my ignorant soul. May I never more question Your existence or omnipotence, which I have this moment so greatly experienced.

Rising from my knees, I went and sat down on the riverbank. My mind was greatly filled with endearing thoughts of that Eternal Goodness who had so remarkably saved me from the dreadful gulf of everlasting ruin just as I was going to plunge myself into it. Now I thought I could not but marvel that I should be so foolish as to call in question the existence of a Deity. Every creature testifies to the existence of its Creator, and man's own conscience, more than a thousand witnesses, cannot but dictate the reality of God to him.

A HEAVENLY VISITOR

While my thoughts were taken up with these meditations as I sat on the riverbank, I was suddenly surrounded with a glorious light. The exceeding brightness was such that I had never seen anything like it before. This both surprised and amazed me. While I was wondering from where it came, I saw coming toward me a glorious appearance. It looked like a man, but it was circled round about with translucent beams of inexpressible light and glory. The rays streamed from him the whole time he came toward me. His countenance was very awe inspiring, yet it was mixed with an air of sweetness that was extremely pleasing. It gave me some secret hopes that he came to me not as an enemy, yet I knew not how to bear his bright appearance.

Endeavoring to stand on my feet, I soon found I had no more strength in me, and so I fell flat down on my face. By the kind assistance of his arm, I was set on my feet again, and new strength was put into me. I soon perceived this new energy and addressed myself to the bright form before me.

Epenetus: O my shining deliverer, who has invigorated my feeble body and restored me to new life, how will I acknowledge my thankfulness, and in what manner will I adore you?

Angel: Pay your adorations to the Author of your being and not to me, who am your fellow creature. I am sent by Him, whose very existence you have so lately denied. I have come to stop you from falling into that eternal ruin wherein you were going to plunge yourself.

This touched my heart with such a sense of my own unworthiness that my soul melted within me, and I could not keep from crying out, "O how utterly unworthy I am of all this grace and mercy!"

Angel: In showing mercy, the Divine Majesty does not consult your unworthiness but His own un-bounded goodness and incomprehensible love. He saw with how much malice the grand Enemy of souls desired your ruin. He let him go on with hopes of overcoming you but still upheld you by His secret power, through which, when Satan thought himself most sure, the snare was broken, and you escaped.

These words made me break forth in ecstatic rapture:

> O who the depths of this great love can tell,
> To save a tempted sinking soul from hell!
> O glory, glory to my Savior's name,
> I'll throughout all eternity proclaim!
> Who, when I on the brink of ruin lay,
> Sav'd me from him who would my soul betray;
> And now I know, though I no God would own,
> The Lord is God, yes, He is God alone!

Angel: Well, so that you may never doubt any more of the reality of eternal things, the purpose of my coming to you is to convince you of the truth of them—not by faith only, but by sight as well. I will show you such things as were never yet seen by mor-tal eye. To that end, your eyes will be strengthened and made capable of beholding immaterial objects.

At these surprising words of the angel, I was much astonished and doubted how I would be able to bear it. I said to him, "O my lord, who is sufficient to endure such a sight?"

To which he replied, *"The joy of the LORD* [will be] *your strength"* (Neh. 8:10). And when he had spoken, he took hold of me. Then he said, "Fear not, for I am sent to show you things you have not seen."

TRANSPORTED TO THE HEAVENS

Before I was aware, I found myself far above the earth, which seemed to me to be a very small and insignificant point in comparison to that region of light into which I was translated.

Then I said to my bright guide, "O let it not offend my lord if I ask a question or two of you."

Angel: Speak on. It is my work to inform you of such things that you will inquire of me, for I am a ministering spirit (Heb. 1:14). I am sent forth to minister to you and to those who will be heirs of salvation.

Epenetus: I would gladly be informed what that dark spot so far below me is. It becomes smaller and smaller as I rise higher and higher and appears much darker since I came into this region of light.

A HEAVENLY PERSPECTIVE OF EARTH

Angel: That little spot that now looks so dark and contemptible is the world of which you were so lately an inhabitant. Here you may see how little all that world appears. Many tirelessly labor and expend all their strength and time to purchase a small part of it.

The earth is subdivided into many kingdoms. To purchase one, so many horrid and base villanies, so many bloody and unnatural murders, have been committed. Yes, this is that spot of earth that to obtain one small part thereof, so many men have run the hazard of losing, no, have actually lost, their precious and immortal souls. These souls are so precious that the Prince of Peace has told us that though one man could gain the whole world, it would not offset so great a loss (Matt. 16:26).

The great reason of their folly is that they do not look to things above. As you well observed as you ascended nearer to this region, the world appeared smaller and yet more contemptible. So it will seem to all who can by faith get their hearts above it. For could the sons of men below but see the world as it is, they would not covet it as they do now; instead, alas, they are in a state of darkness.

What is even worse is that they love to walk therein. For though the Prince of Light came down among them and plainly showed them the true *"light of life"* (John 8:12), which by His ministers He still continues to do, yet they go on in their darkness and will not bring themselves into the light because their deeds are evil, and they love the darkness (John 3:19).

CONDEMNATION OF THE FALLEN ANGELS

Epenetus: What were those multitudes of black and horrid forms that hover in the air above the world? I indeed would have been very afraid of them, but I saw that as you passed by, they fled, perhaps not being able to endure the brightness with which you are clothed.

Angel: They were the fallen and apostate spirits, who for their pride and rebellion were cast down from heaven and wander in the air by the decree of the Almighty. They are bound in chains of darkness and kept until the judgment of the Great Day. From there, they are permitted to descend into the world, both for the trial of the elect and for the condemnation of the wicked. And though you now see they have black and horrid forms, yet they were once the sons of light and were arrayed in robes of glorious brightness like what you see we wear. The loss of which, though it was the result of their own willful sin, fills them with rage and malice against the ever blessed God whose power and majesty they fear and hate. Having lost their innocence and glory, they flee from those spirits that have kept their station and still continue their obedience to their great Creator.

Epenetus: But tell me, O my happy guide, have these unfaithful spirits no hope of being reconciled to God again, after some term of time, or at least some of them?

Angel: No, not at all. They are lost forever. They were the first who sinned and had no Tempter, and they were immediately cast down from heaven. In addition, the Son of God, the blessed Messiah, by whom alone salvation can be had, took not the angelic nature, but left the apostate angels all to perish. He only took on Himself the seed of Abraham. For this reason, they have so much malice against the sons of men, whom it is a torment to them to see made heirs of heaven while they are doomed to hell.

THE RESPLENDENT BEAUTY OF THE SUN AND STARS

By this time, we had gone above the sun, whose vast and glorious body, more than a hundred times greater than the earth, moved around the great expanse wherein it was placed with such a mighty swiftness that to relate it would appear incredible. My guide told me this mighty, immense hanging globe of fire was one of the great works of God. It moves with so swift a motion, more than a hundred thousand miles in that small space of time we call an hour, and yet it always keeps its constant course. It never has the least irregularity in its daily or its annual motion. It is so exceedingly glorious in its body that if my sight had not been greatly strengthened, I could not have beheld it.

Nor were those mighty globes of fire we call the fixed stars less wonderful. Their vast and extreme height, at least ten thousand leagues above the sun, makes them appear like candles in our sight, though every one of them exceeds in magnitude the body of the earth. Should but one of those vast bodies fall on the earth, it would burn the world to cinders in a moment. Yet they hang within their spheres without any support, in a pure sea of ether, so thin, so ethereal that nothing but His Word, which first created them, could keep them in their places.

CREATION WITNESSES TO THE POWER OF ITS CREATOR

Epenetus: These wonders are enough to convince anyone of the great power of their loving Creator and of the blackness of that infidel who can call in question the existence of God, who has given the whole world so many clear evidences of His power and glory. If men were not like beasts, still looking downward, they could not help but acknowledge His great power and wisdom.

Angel: You speak what is true, but you will see far greater things than these. These are but the scaffolds and remote outer constructions to that glorious building where the blessed above inhabit, that *"house not made with hands, eternal in the heavens"* (2 Cor. 5:1), a view of which, as far as you are capable to comprehend it, will now be shown to you.

4

Visions of Heaven and the Glory Thereof

What I had been told by my guide, I found to be true in a few moments, for I was presently translated into the glorious mansions of the blessed. The things I saw are impossible to describe, and the ravishing melodious harmony I heard, I can never express. The beloved apostle John said it well in his epistle: *"Now are we the sons of God, and it doth not yet appear what we shall be"* (1 John 3:2). Whoever has not seen that glory can speak but very imperfectly of it, and those who have cannot tell the thousandth part of what it is. Therefore, the great Apostle of the Gentiles, who tells us he had been caught up into paradise where he had heard unspeakable words that are not possible for a man to utter (2 Cor. 12:4), gives us no other account of it but that *"eye hath not seen, nor ear heard, neither have entered into the heart of man, the things which God hath prepared for them that love him"* (1 Cor. 2:9). But I will give you the best account I can of what I saw and heard and of the discourses I had with some of the blessed.

THE SOURCE OF ALL LIGHT

When I was first brought near this glorious place, I saw innumerable hosts of bright attendants, who welcomed me into that blissful seat of happiness, having in all their countenances an air of perfect joy and highest satisfaction. There I saw that perfect and unapproachable light that assimilates all things into its own nature, for even the souls of the glorified saints are transparent and ethereal. Neither are they illuminated by the sun or any created luminaries. All that light, which flows with so much transparent brightness throughout those heavenly mansions, is nothing but emanations of the divine glory. In comparison, the light of the sun is but darkness. And all the luster of the most sparkling diamonds, the fire of garnets, sapphires, and rubies, and the orient brightness of the richest pearls are like dead coals in comparison to its glory. Called the throne of the God of glory, the radiant luster of the Divine Majesty is revealed in the most illustrious manner.

The indescribable Deity, exalted on the high throne of His glory, receiving the adorations of myriads of angels and saints who sing forth eternal hallelujahs and praises to Him, was too bright an object for humankind to view. Therefore, He may well be called the God of glory, for by His glorious presence, He makes heaven what it is. Rivers of pleasure, tranquil cheerfulness, joy, and splendor perpetually spring from the Divine Presence to all the blessed inhabitants of heaven, the place of His happy residence and seat of His eternal empire. The Divine Majesty scatters the richest beams of His goodness and glory, and His chosen saints and servants see and praise His everlasting, dear perfection.

For my own part, my sight was far too weak to bear the least transparent ray shot from that everlasting Spring of light and glory, who sat upon the throne. I was forced to cry to my guide, "The sight of so much glory is too great for frail humankind to bear, yet it is so refreshing and delightful that I would willingly behold it though I die!"

NO PLACE FOR SIN AND SORROW

Angel: No, no, death does not enter within this blessed place. Here life and immortality reside. Neither sin nor sorrow have anything to do here, for it is the glory of this happy place to be forever freed from all that is evil. Without that exemption, our blessedness even here would be imperfect. But come along with me, and I will lead you to one who is in the body, as you are. Converse with him awhile until I send another ministering spirit.

Epenetus: Instead, let me stay here, for there is no need for building tabernacles; the heavenly mansions are already fitted.

To which my shining messenger replied, "In a while, you will be secure forever, but the divine will must be obeyed first."

CONVERSATION WITH ELIJAH

Swift as a thought, he presently conveyed me through thousands of those bright and winged spirits. Then he presented me to that illustrious saint, the great Elijah, who lived in the world below so many hundreds of ages past and gone, yet I thought I knew him at first sight as well as if we had been contemporaries.

Angel: Here is one (said my guide to Elijah) who by commission from the imperial throne has been permitted to survey these realms of light. I have brought him here to learn from you wherein its glory and happiness consist.

Elijah: That I will gladly do, for it is our meat and drink in these blessed regions to do the will of God and of the Lamb (see John 4:34), to sing His praise, and to serve Him with the humblest adoration, saying, *"Blessing, and honour, and glory, and power, be unto him that sitteth upon the throne, and unto the Lamb for ever and ever"* (Rev. 5:13). He *"hast redeemed us to God by* [His] *blood out of every kindred, and tongue, and people, and nation; and hast made us unto our God kings and priests"* (vv. 9–10). *"Even so, Amen"* (Rev. 1:7).

Likewise, I added my Amen to that of the holy prophet. The prophet then inquired how this great permission and privilege had been given to me. I understand the saints in heaven are ignorant of what is done on earth. How then can prayers be directed to them?

I then related what I have here set down by way of introduction. Then the holy prophet broke forth into this exclamation:

Elijah: Glory forever be ascribed to Him who sits upon the throne and to the Lamb for His unbounded goodness and great condescension to the weakness of a poor, doubting sinner. Now give attention to what I will speak.

Elijah Describes His Spiritual Body

Elijah: What you have seen and heard already, I am sure you never can relate so as to make it understood, for *"eye hath not seen, nor ear heard, neither have entered into the heart of man, the things which God hath prepared for them that love him"* (1 Cor. 2:9). I am referring to those not yet translated to this glorious state or freed from their physical bodies. Nor is my presence in the body here any objection to what I now assert. For though my body has not been subject to the common lot of mortals—death—yet it has suffered such a change as has been in some sense equivalent to physical death. It is

43

made both spiritual and impenetrable and is now no more capable of any further suffering than those blessed angels are who surround the throne. Yet in this consummate state of happiness, I cannot express all that I enjoy, nor do I know what will yet be enjoyed, for here our happiness is always new.

Heaven's Happiness Is Perfect

I then requested of the blessed prophet to explain himself a little more because I did not understand how happiness could be absolutely perfect and yet admit new additions. For in the world below, we generally think that what is perfect is completely finished.

Epenetus: I humbly hope that what I will say may not be taken as the result of a vain curiosity. My desire is only that my understanding may be cultivated, which yet retains but dark ideas of these heavenly things.

Elijah: To satisfy your doubting soul and to confirm your wavering faith are the chief reasons for your being brought here through the permission of the great Trinity; therefore, if any doubt arises in your mind, I would have you make it known. But as for your question that happiness cannot be complete and yet admit new additions, I must tell you that when the soul and body both are happy, as mine are now, I count it a consummate state of happiness.

Through all the innumerable ages of eternity, the soul and body, joined together in the blessed resurrection state, will forever be the subjects of this happiness. But in respect to the blessed object of this happiness, which is the ever worthy and blessed God in whose vision this happiness consists, it is forever new. The divine perfections are infinite. Nothing less than eternity can be sufficient to display their glory, which makes our happiness eternally allow new additions; moreover, by a necessary consequence, our knowledge of this happiness will be eternally progressive too.

Paul's Response to His Heavenly Vision

Elijah: Therefore, it was not without reason that the great Apostle of the Gentiles, who in the days of his mortality was once admitted here as you are, affirmed: *"Eye hath not seen, nor ear heard, neither have entered into the heart of man, the things which God hath prepared for them that love him"* (1 Cor. 2:9).

Heaven's Sights beyond Description

Elijah: The eyes have seen many admirable things in nature. They have seen mountains of crystal and rocks of diamonds. They have seen mines of gold, coasts of pearl, and spicy islands, yet the eyes that have seen so many wonders in the world below could never pry into the glories of this triumphant state.

Heaven's Sounds Defy Comparison

Elijah: And though the ears of man have heard many delightful and harmonious sounds, even all that art and nature could supply, yet they have never heard the heavenly melody that here both saints and angels make before the throne.

Heaven Is beyond Conception

Elijah: As the eye has not seen nor the ear heard, so neither can the heart of man conceive the glories of heaven (1 Cor. 2:9). The heart of man, the chief work of the all-wise Creator, is of so fine and careful composition that it can almost envision anything that either is, was, or ever will be in the world below—even what will never be.

Man can imagine that every stone on earth will be turned into pearls of great luster and every blade of grass into the brightest and shiniest of jewels. He can conceive that every particle of dust will be turned into silver and the whole earth into a mass of pure refined gold. He can imagine the air turned into crystal, every star advanced into a sun, and every sun made a thousand times larger and more glorious than what it now appears to be, yet this is infinitely short of what the High Eternal Majesty, who is incomprehensible in all His works of wonder, has prepared for all His faithful followers here. (See 1 Corinthians 2:9.)

WHAT THE BLESSED ARE DELIVERED FROM

Elijah: In order for you to possess the best idea of our happiness, I will briefly describe to you what it is those blessed souls, who through the glorious purchase of our bright Redeemer are brought here, are delivered from. Ages spent on this delightful theme would scarcely suffice to tell it to you fully. So that you may better understand it, I will endeavor to conform my words to your capacity by comparing things that are above to what you know below, although your eyes have told you how heavenly things infinitely transcend whatever can be found on earth.

Freed from Sin's Misery

Elijah: First then, the souls of all the blessed here are freed forever from whatever it is that can make them miserable; the chief of which, you are not unaware, is sin. It is only that which brings the creature into misery and imposes it on him. At first, the blessed God made all things happy, all like Himself, who is supremely so. Had sin not defaced the beauty of heaven's workmanship, neither angels nor men would ever have known what is meant by misery. It was sin that threw the apostate angels down to hell and spoiled the beauty of the lower world. It was sin that defaced God's image in man's soul and made the lord of the creation a slave to his own lust. By doing so, he plunged himself into an ocean of eternal misery from which there was no redemption.

It is an invaluable mercy that in this happy place all the inhabitants are freed, forever freed, from sin through the blood of our redeeming Jesus, to whom blessing, honor, power, glory, and eternal praises be ascribed forever.

Below, the best and holiest of souls groan underneath the burden of corruption. Sin cleaves to all they do and leads them captive often against their wills. *"Who shall deliver me?"* (Rom. 7:24) has been the cry of many of God's faithful servants, who at the same time have been dear to Jesus. Sin is the heavy impediment of even saints while they are embodied in corrupted flesh; therefore, when they lay their bodies down, their souls are like birds loosed from their cages. With a heavenly vigor, they mount up to this blessed region, triumphing over sin, with which below they still maintained a combat. But here, their warfare is at an end, and *"death is swallowed up in victory"* (1 Cor. 15:54). Here their bright souls, which were deformed and stained by sin, are presented without *"spot, or wrinkle"* (Eph. 5:27) to the eternal Father by the ever blessed Jesus.

Freed from Sin's Temptations

Elijah: Secondly, as here the blessed souls are freed from sin, so are they likewise freed from all opportunity to sin, which is a great addition to their happiness. In Paradise in his original creation, Adam thought he was perfectly innocent and freed from sin, yet he was not freed from temptations to it, which was his great unhappiness. Satan got into Paradise to tempt him, and he fatally yielded to the Devil's temptations. He ate of the forbidden fruit and fell, and by his fall, human nature, and consequently his posterity, are all corrupted.

Sin, like a gangrene, entered human nature and corrupted all humankind. And that corruption, which every mortal harbors in his heart, is a most dangerous and frequently prevailing tempter. But here, each blessed soul is likewise freed from this. No devil can tempt anyone here, nor can any corruption enter. Nothing but what is pure and holy can find admission here. No sly suggestions from an apostate spirit can molest us here. That *"roaring lion"* (1 Pet. 5:8), which below is in constant motion, traversing the earth and *"seeking whom he may devour"* (v. 8), is, with respect to us in this blessed region of life and immortality, bound fast in everlasting chains, shut up safe in an infernal prison, and doomed to the vengeance of eternal fire.

Nor will the world, which by the fall of man has lost its beauty and is degenerated into emptiness and vanity and does by its bewitching charms and false allurements draw thousands to perdition, be any more a tempter to those blessed souls who have, *"through faith and patience"* (Heb. 6:12), overcome its wiles and arrived safely here.

As strong as its temptations and allurements are to saints themselves, who are still struggling with it in the world below, we here who are possessed of heavenly mansions look with contempt on all earthly enjoyments. We here have overcome the world and all that it can tempt us with. Through the blood of our triumphing Jesus, we have won the victory over it, as those bright palms we bear do evidence (Rev. 7:9). There is nothing here that can disturb our peace, but an eternal calm crowns all our happiness since we are freed from sin and all temptations to it.

Freed from Sin's Consequences

Elijah: Thirdly, here we are freed from the effects of sin, and that is the punishment that those who are confined to the dark regions of eternal misery are ever groaning under. It is what they cannot bear, yet what they must suffer forever. It was sin that ushered death into the world below. As every mortal finds, death is the just wages of sin by heaven's high decree (Rom. 6:23). But through the conquest of the Prince of Life, the Lamb of God slain from the world's foundation (Rev. 13:8), sin, death, and hell are banished forever from this place. By His dying, He overcame both death and him who had the power thereof, the Devil (Heb. 2:14). He triumphed over sin, death, and hell, for which eternal songs of praise and victory are ever offered to His holy name.

WHAT THE BLESSED ENJOY

Elijah: These are the things that we in this blessed state are delivered from, yet these make up but the least part of the happiness of heaven. Our

50

joys are positive, as well as personal. I will describe them to the extent that your understanding can grasp.

Seeing God Face to Face

Elijah: We here enjoy the beautiful vision, the blessed Spring and eternal Source of all our happiness. What this is I can no more declare than finite creatures can comprehend infinity. We find that it continually enlightens our understandings and fills our souls *"with joy unspeakable and full of glory"* (1 Pet. 1:8). His love will be inexhaustible throughout eternity, and nothing but the blessed Author of it can satisfy. It is the reflecting brightness of the Divine Presence and transcendently glorious emanations of His goodness that is the Life of our lives, the Soul of our souls, and the Heaven of heaven. It is what makes us live, love, sing, and praise forever. It transforms our souls into His blessed likeness.

The saints below, while they are traveling toward this blessed country, are supported by His *"everlasting arms"* (Deut. 33:27), by which they are enabled to go from grace to grace. But we who are safely landed on the haven of eternal happiness *"are changed into the same image from glory to glory, even as by the Spirit of the Lord"* (2 Cor. 3:18).

But to bring things nearer to your understanding, by thus looking at God's face, we have a real participation and enjoyment of His love, and His blessed smile makes our souls glad. We rejoice continually in His favor, for in His favor is life (Ps.

51

30:5). Then by this blessed vision of God, we come to know Him beyond what anyone did below, for it is the sight of Him that illuminates our understandings and gives us *"the light of the knowledge of the glory of God in the face of Jesus Christ"* (2 Cor. 4:6). Although it is impossible to comprehend the Divine Majesty—for who can truly know the Almighty to perfection?—yet here we have a perfect understanding of His nature and divine attributes.

Communion with God

Elijah: Here we have not only the blessed vision whereby we see God as He is, but also a real enjoyment of Him. Thereby, we come to be united to Him and to live in Him and He in us (1 John 4:13). We come to be *"partakers of the divine nature"* (2 Pet. 1:4), which shines forth in us with a resplendent brightness. In the world below, the saints do indeed enjoy God in His ordinances, but here we all enjoy Him face-to-face. Below, the saints enjoy God in part, but here we enjoy Him without measure. There they have some sips of His goodness, but here we have an abundance. We swim in the boundless ocean of happiness. Below, the saints' communion with God is many times broken off and discontinued, but here we have an uninterrupted enjoyment of God without intermission or cessation.

The Fullness of God's Gifts

Elijah: Here we enjoy the perfection of all grace. In the world below, the saints see but in part and know but in part; but here, what is perfect is enjoyed, and what is imperfect has been done away with (1 Cor. 13:9–10). Below, love is mixed with fear, and *"fear hath torment"* (1 John 4:18), but here, love is perfect, and *"perfect love casteth out fear"* (v. 18).

Here we love the blessed God more than ourselves and one another like ourselves. We are all the children of one Father, and all our brothers and sisters are dear to us. Below, our love was still divided and ran in several channels, but here our love has but one stream and centers in the ever blessed God, the Fountain of our happiness.

Likewise, our knowledge in the world below was very imperfect, seeing but darkly as through a broken mirror, but here we see God as He is, and so we come to know Him as we are known (1 Cor. 13:12). Here, our joy is perfect. In the world below, it was interrupted by sorrow and sighing. It was necessarily so, for where there is sin, there will be sorrow. But here, all sin, the cause of sorrow, is banished; all sorrow, the result of sin, is ceased. In fact, through the bounty of our blessed Redeemer, our very sorrow for sin when on the earth increases our joy now that we are here.

Unlimited Capacity

Elijah: Here we have our capacities enlarged, according to the greatness of the objects we have to contemplate. While we were in the world below, no light could shine into our minds except through the windows of our senses. Therefore, the blessed God was pleased to condescend to our capacities and to adapt the expressions of His Majesty to the narrowness of our imaginations. But here, the revelation of the Deity is much more glorious, and our minds are clarified from all those earthly images that flow through the unrefined channels of the senses.

A Clearer Vision

Elijah: Below, our purest conceptions of God were very imperfect, but here, the gold is separated from the dross, and our conceptions are more proper and befitting the simplicity and purity of God. Below, the objects of glory were humbled to the perceptions of sense, but here, the sensible faculties are raised, refined, and made the subjects of glory. Now that the divine light shines with direct beams, and the thick curtains of flesh are spiritualized and transparent, the soul enjoys the clearest vision of God.

We now see what before we believed of the glorious nature of the ever blessed God: His decrees and counsels, His providence and dispensations. We clearly see that from eternity, God was sole existing, but not solitary; that the Godhead is neither confused in unity nor divided in number; that there is a priority of order, but no superiority among the sacred persons of the indescribable Trinity, but that they are equally possessed of the same divine excellencies and the same divine empire and are equally the object of the same divine adoration.

Those ways of God that below seemed unsearchable, and that we thought unlawful to inquire into, we here perceive to be the product of divine wisdom, with so much perspicuity and clearness that truth itself is not more evident. These things are some of those blessings that constitute our happiness.

THE QUALITIES OF THE SPIRITUAL BODY

Elijah: All these things are only what relate to our souls, but still, the happiness of the inhabitants of this blessed region will not be complete until their bodies are raised and reunited to their souls. Through divine generosity, the blessed Enoch and I enjoy a more peculiar preference, being translated here in the body as types—both to the anti- and postdiluvian [before and after the flood] world—of the resurrection of the ever worthy Son of God and of all the saints through Him. Because as yet, none but the great Messiah has been actually raised from the dead, He is the firstfruits thereof (1 Cor. 15:23). As for Enoch and myself, our bodies have not known death, though they have received a change equivalent thereto. Therefore, it is more difficult to declare what the resurrection state will be. It is to be discerned in its perfection only from His glorious body, to which neither that of Enoch's nor mine are comparable in respect to the glory thereof, though both are spiritual bodies. I will now show you the distinct properties of resurrected bodies.

Spiritual but Substantial

Elijah: At the Resurrection, the bodies of the blessed here will be, as mine is now, spiritual bodies. By your not only seeing, but touching me (at which the holy prophet was pleased to give me his hand), you may be better able to know what I mean by a spiritual body, that is, a body rarefied from all coarse mixtures of corruption and made pure and refined, yet substantial; it is not composed of wind and air as mortals below are apt to imagine.

Here I asked the holy prophet to bear with me. I informed him that I had always understood spiritual as that which is the opposite of material; consequently, I thought that a spiritual body must be immaterial, thus not capable of being felt as I found his was.

To this the prophet replied that their bodies were spiritual, not only as they were purified from all corruption, but as they were sustained by the enjoyment of God without any material refreshments, such as meat, drink, sleep, and clothing, which were supports to our bodies below.

Elijah: Have you not read that after His resurrection, the blessed Jesus appeared in His body to His disciples when they met together in a chamber, though the doors were shut about them? This plainly evinces the lack of material substance to His body, yet he invited Thomas to come and reach out his hand and thrust it into His side, which shows it plainly to be substantial. Both our souls and bodies live on and are supported forever by this blissful vision.

Eternal

Elijah: Our bodies in the resurrection state will be immortal and incapable of dying. Below, their bodies are all mortal, dying and perishing, and subject to be crumbled into dust every moment. But here, our bodies will be incorruptible and freed from death forever. Our corruption will put on incorruption *"that mortality might be swallowed up of life"* (2 Cor. 5:4).

Here I desired the prophet to bear with me a little while I gave him an account of my own notions in this matter.

Elijah: Say on, for I am ready to resolve your doubt.

Epenetus: I have learned in the Holy Scriptures that immortality is an attribute that belongs to God only and not to men, especially to the bodies of men, which everyday experience tells us are mortal. Therefore, St. Paul tells Timothy that God alone has immortality (1 Tim. 6:16).

Elijah: When I say the bodies of the blessed here are immortal, I am referring to the bodies in their raised state. Then they are subject to death no more. Man in his corruptible state is mortal and subject to death. There is nothing more evident to all who dwell in the world below. At this time, even the bodies of all these glorified souls who are here are kept under the power of death. But in the resurrection state when they will be raised, they will then be immortal.

As to what you mention from the Scripture, that only the blessed God has immortality, it is very true. He is most eminently and essentially so, whereas there is no creature, neither angel nor man, who can in that strict sense be said to be so. We are immortal through His grace and favor, but God is immortal in His essence and has been so from all eternity. In that sense, He may well be said to alone have immortality. Therefore, it will not be amiss for you to observe that whatever the blessed God is, He is eminently and essentially so; in which respect, it is likewise said of Him that He alone is holy, and there is *"none good but one, that is, God"* (Matt. 19:17). There is none righteous, nor none more merciful than He to whom be *"blessing, and glory, and wisdom, and thanksgiving, and honour, and power, and might...for ever and ever"* (Rev. 7:12).

Resurrected

Epenetus: I have one thing more to be satisfied about. Seeing there is only yourself and the prophet Enoch who are permitted to be here in the body, which you are pleased to say has suffered a change equivalent to death, but died not, what assurance do you have that the bodies of the blessed that are now under the power of death will be raised again? For I see they are gloriously blessed and happy without their bodies and seem not to have any need for them.

They have long since perished and rotted in their graves. The greatest thing that I think can be said for it is that the ever blessed Jesus, the spotless Lamb of God, who was truly and really dead, is now alive and lives forevermore.

To this the prophet, interrupting me, replied, "What greater proof can you desire than this?"

Epenetus: What I have to say to that is that the body of the blessed Jesus never saw corruption, and that there is no instance of any body that ever saw corruption that was yet raised to life and immortality.

Elijah: Although it is true there has been no such instance, yet the resurrection of the body is as sure as the present glorification of the soul. For as the blessed Jesus died as a public person, so did He also rise again; therefore, He is said to be the firstfruits from the dead (1 Cor. 15:20–23). He is the Head of the church (Eph. 1:22) and cannot be complete without the members of His body, who in their order will be raised up to be with Him forever. The body will be awakened out of its dead sleep, and as I was saying, quickened into a glorious, immortal life.

The body, in addition to the soul, is an essential part of man. Though the inequality is great in their holy operations, their concurrence is necessary. Good actions in the world below are indeed designed by the counsel and resolution of the soul but performed by the ministry of the body. Every grace expresses itself in visible actions thereby.

In the sorrows of repentance, tears were supplied by the eyes. In thanksgiving, the tongue was used to break forth in the praises of God. All the victories over pleasure and pain below were obtained by the soul in conjunction with the body. And can you think that the Divine Goodness will deal so differently with them that the soul should be everlastingly happy and the body be lost in forgetfulness? Should the one be glorified in heaven while the other remains in the dust?

From their first beginnings in the world below until the grave, they both ran the same race and therefore will enjoy the same reward. When the crown of righteousness and glory (2 Tim. 4:8) will be given to the blessed at the Great Day in the view of all, both soul and body will partake of the honor thereof. And this is, I believe, enough to satisfy your doubt as to the resurrection of the body.

To which I replied that I had nothing further to object to in that particular question. Then I desired that he would go on in describing the glory of the body in the resurrection state. Upon which, the prophet thus proceeded:

Immortal

Elijah: I have already told you that the bodies of the blessed will be immortal, but they cannot be as immortal as God is, who is so eminently and essentially so that, as you well observed, He alone is said to have immortality. Nor yet are they immortal in the same sense as the blessed angels are, who being immaterial substances are so created; whereas man has his immortality through the purchase of the blessed Jesus and the renovation of the divine image. Nor can we compare the immortality thus purchased for us to that of the apostate spirits, who are immortal too; theirs is with such an immortality as brings along with it a greater weight of misery. Their immortality is such a curse as makes them wish a million times that they might be annihilated. But that blessed immortality that we enjoy is the happiness of heaven, and therefore rightly called a glorious immortality. It gives us an assurance that the happiness we now enjoy, we will enjoy forever.

Impenetrable

Elijah: Another happiness the bodies of the blessed here enjoy is that they are impenetrable, so they are incapable of experiencing sufferings. Below, the bodies of the saints oftentimes become like many shops of misery or like a hospital full of diseases, which are the common harbingers of death. When they are not so, sometimes they suffer something worse than death. At times, the pains and infirmities of their bodies are such that death appears much more desirable than such a life. How many times are even good men racked with gout or tortured by kidney stones with the most exquisite and excruciating pain? Although they abound in the fullness of all those things that mortals count the blessings of the life below, yet they are thereby embittered to them by those tormenting pains that have seized their bodies.

Where wracking pain is not present, but men have healthy, strong, and vigorous bodies, they often meet with other sufferings and are exposed to hunger, thirst, cold, and nakedness, which make their lives very uncomfortable. Many times, they are shut up in prison, enclosed within stone walls, and are, as it were, buried while they are still alive. They are as men forgotten in the world. Considering all these things, their bodies are miserable while on the earth below.

But in these happy regions, there are no such evils that can attack them. Here their condition is extremely different. No curse can enter here. All those things I have related are only the effects of sin. My body is incapable of suffering any evil, either of sin or sorrow. On the contrary, through the grace of the blessed Son of God, it is now become a receptacle both of light and glory, and so will all the bodies of the saints be likewise in their resurrection state. This leads me to declare the fourth endowment with which our bodies will ever be blessed.

Beautiful

Elijah: Another happiness our bodies will enjoy in the blessed resurrection state is that they will be truly beautiful. This is not the least of our privileges. For below, our bodies are but vile bodies, tending to corruption. In the grave, worms gnaw and feed on their flesh, and thence proceeds a loathsome odor. At best, they are but houses of clay, and their foundation is in the dust.

But here, it will be otherwise, for the bodies of the saints will be freed from innocent infirmities that were inseparable from Adam in Paradise, whose soul united to the body was the fountain of the natural, sensitive life. Being in a perpetual flux, there was the necessity for continual repairs to preserve his life in vigor, whereas in this blessed state, the body will be spiritual in its qualities, and the principle of its life supported by the supernatural power of the Spirit, without outward nourishment.

Not only so, but a substantial and unfading glory will shine in them, infinitely above the perishing pride of this world and the glory of the flesh. They will be made like the glorious body of Christ, who will change our vile bodies so that they may be fashioned like His glorious body (Phil. 3:21). He will do this according to the working of that mighty power, whereby He is able to subdue all things to Himself (Eph. 1:19-22).

This transcendent beauty that He will put on the body will be the work of His own hands, and where Omnipotence intervenes, nothing is difficult. The beautifying of a raised body and putting it into an immortal state of glory is as easy to the Divine Power as the first framing of it in the womb.

Agile

Elijah: Another part of our happiness is that our bodies will be agile and move with an inconceivable swiftness. While below, our bodies are awkward and heavy and are as weights to the soul. But in the raised state, it will be otherwise. Our bodies will be like the *"chariots of Amminadib"* (Song 6:12) and move far swifter than the winged fowls in the aerial heavens.

Pure

Elijah: Another thing in which our happiness will very much consist is that our bodies then, as mine is now, will all be pure. This is an exceeding privilege, for though they should have all the other aforementioned qualities and be immortal, spiritual, impenetrable, beautiful, and swift, yet if they still were sinful, it would blemish all the rest. If sin could enter heaven, it would even spoil the happiness we here enjoy. But it is far otherwise.

Our glory is that here our very bodies will be pure and have no spot of sin on them at all. Below, indeed, the bodies of the saints are burdened with sin and shackled with temptations, which makes them cry out, *"O wretched man that I am! who shall deliver me from the body of this death?"* (Rom. 7:24). But here they will enjoy that blessed redemption of their bodies, which they wait for there.

Glorious

Elijah: To conclude, the bodies of the saints in their resurrection state will be glorious bodies. They will be so splendid that they will have a close resemblance to the glorious body of our blessed Redeemer. The Divine Oracles inform us how this will be achieved: the glorious Lamb of God, the blessed Jesus, will change our vile and corruptible bodies and make them like His own. It is by His power that the saints' bodies, *"sown in corruption"* (1 Cor. 15:42) and *"in dishonour"* [will be] *raised in glory"* (v. 43). In that blessed resurrection state, they will shine more brightly than the sun in this triumphant kingdom of their Father.

And thus, my son, I have informed you briefly wherein the glory and the happiness of this blessed state we here enjoy consists. Not that I have said the thousandth part of what might be further still related—nor could you understand it if I would. For there are some things here that we enjoy, like the white stone on which is written the new name, and no one knows it but those who receive it (Rev. 2:17).

When the holy prophet concluded his remarks, I humbly thanked him for the information he had given me. I told him that though I was incapable—clothed as I was with such a lump of unrefined flesh—of understanding all I had heard or of speaking about what I saw, yet I had seen and heard enough forever to convince me both of the excellency and reality of heavenly things, which in the world below so many question and so few believe.

THE PERFECT KNOWLEDGE OF THE BLESSED

Epenetus: But let it not offend my lord if I desire yet further to be resolved in some few things.

Elijah: Speak, and I will endeavor to give you satisfaction.

Epenetus: The first thing I would humbly ask is how the blessed here, who are but creatures, though thus glorified, and therefore finite still, can have so perfect an idea of the incomprehensible and infinite Three One, to know Him so as we ourselves are known, as you before affirmed, or did I in my weakness misunderstand you?

Elijah: In saying so, I did affirm no more than what the Sacred Oracles contain. For the Apostle of the Gentiles, speaking in the days of his flesh to them who then inhabited the world below, told them that they then saw *"through a glass, darkly,"* but that in these bright regions, they would see Him *"face to face"* (1 Cor. 13:12); that he himself knew but *"in part,"* but that once he got here, he would know even as he was known (v. 12).

But, my son, these words are not to be understood according to the exactness of the expression, for the sun that lights the lower world may as well be included in a small spark of fire as the incomprehensible and infinite God may be comprehended by our finite faculties. Beyond the fullest discoveries we can possibly make of the Deity, there remains still an entire infinity of perfections, the knowledge whereof is altogether unattainable by the most intelligent of all those glorious spirits that are the bright and continual attendants of the throne.

That expression, "as we are known" (see 1 Corinthians 13:12), which gave you an occasion to inquire into the sense of it, is to be taken as a note of comparison and not of equality. The dim light of a candle shines as truly as the bright luminary of the day but not with the same extent and splendor.

Therefore, the sum of what I can say to this point is that we have here as perfect a knowledge of the blessed God as created beings are capable of receiving or our own hearts of desiring.

I then returned my humble thanks to the great prophet and assured him that his answer had entirely satisfied me. I found it was only the deficiency of my own understanding that had caused any trouble for him.

Elijah: You still mistake the state that I am in, for there is no such thing as trouble here, nor can there be. For the spreading of the knowledge of the ever blessed God, proclaiming His bright eternal excellencies, and displaying His glory are those things that give the blessed here the greatest satisfaction and delight. They will ever do so throughout the numerous ages of eternity.

Then, with an air of greater confidence, I told the holy prophet that I had yet another question to ask him.

Elijah: Say on, and I will answer you.

DIFFERENT DEGREES OF GLORY

Epenetus: Among the many blessed souls I passed by as my bright messenger led me to you, I saw some who appeared to me to shine with greater brightness than the others, which gave me a desire to be informed whether or not there are among the blessed different degrees of glory.

Elijah: The happiness and glory, which all the saints here enjoy, are the result of their communion with and love for the ever holy God, whose blessed vision here, as I have said before, is the eternal spring from which it flows. The more we see, the more we love, and love assimilates our souls into the nature of the blessed object of it. From that place, our glory proceeds.

Therefore, this make a difference in the degrees thereof. It is not as though there were any lack of love to God in any of the blessed here, for that is impossible. There is not one soul among the numerous inhabitants of this bright region who does not adore and love the ever blessed God with all his utmost powers and faculties. It follows then that as those powers and faculties are different, their love must be so, too; consequently, so is their glory.

Nor is there any murmuring or repining in one to see another's glory much greater than his own, but God is thereby magnified the more as the eternal Source of all their happiness. Nor can there be room for a thought to think it otherwise. Who can complain when all the faculties of each blessed soul are so replenished with the bright emanations of the Deity that they can hold no more? The ever blessed God is an unbounded ocean of light and life, joy and happiness, still filling every vessel that is put therein until it can hold no more. And though the vessels are of several sizes, while each is filled, there is none that can complain.

Besides, each blessed soul here is fashioned not only to a submission, but to such a satisfaction and complacency in the divine good pleasure that all his happiness consists therein. Thus, though the stars below are each one glorious, yet since they are of different magnitudes, one star exceeds another star in glory; and so, as the Divine Oracles inform you, it will be in the resurrection state (1 Cor. 15:41–42).

My answer, therefore, to your question is that those who have the most enlarged faculties do love God most and are thereby assimilated most into His likeness, which is the highest glory heaven can give. Nor let this seem strange to you, for even among God's flaming ministers (Ps. 104:4), the blessed angels, there are diversities of orders and different degrees of glory. And these perhaps were some of those whom you saw as you came here.

While I was thus discoursing with the holy prophet, and with delight heard the solution of those doubts that I desired to be resolved in, a shining form approached me, saying, "How! Epenetus here!"

REUNION WITH A FRIEND

I was surprised to hear my name thus mentioned, and turning suddenly about, I soon perceived it was the noble Junius, my late deceased friend, who approached me.

Junius: Dear Epenetus, I am glad to see you in these blessed regions but am surprised to see you here not yet divested of mortality. Tell me, friend, by what means you came here, and also how it was that you obtained this privilege, for the unusualness of such a thing is what makes me so inquisitive.

I was so overjoyed to see one of my old friends, one with whom I had been so familiar in the world. I tried to embrace him in my arms, which he refused. He told me gently that he had some time ago laid down his body, which he had left below, resting in hope until the Resurrection. (See 1 Peter 1:3–5.) Although he was still indeed a substance, it was an immaterial one, not to be touched by mortals.

Junius: But how did you come to be brought here in your mortal and unchanged body?

I then related to him my temptation and deliverance, which I had told at large in the prefixed introduction to this vision before I had spoken with Elijah.

Junius: Well, Epenetus, I see then there was need enough for the order to be sent forth in the poor world below after my death. There was a need for a lecture to evidence the existence of a Deity, against a sort of men far worse than those in hell, who both believe the existence of God and tremble at His justice.

But you, my friend, who had so long made a profession of His truth and had such great experience of His goodness that you should after all be brought to question His being and existence was indeed something more than ordinary, and what I hardly could have ever thought. It gives me fresh occasion to adore the ever blessed God, who through His abundant goodness has now delivered me from all those snares the Enemy of souls was laying for me and thus preserved me to His heavenly kingdom. Blessed forever be His holy name.

ELIJAH DEPARTS

The blessed Elijah, having heard what Junius said, told me he would leave me now to my friend, and before I was aware of it, the prophet winged away. When he left us, I addressed myself to my noble friend.

CONVERSATION WITH JUNIUS

Epenetus: I could not doubt, my dearest Junius, but that you were one of the blessed inhabitants of this happy region, for such a bright and flaming zeal as that which in the world made you so eminent must of necessity meet with a suitable reward.

Junius: O Epenetus, were you but once divested of mortality, you would have other thoughts than what you have. You would then see how those who have done their utmost in the world below fall infinitely short of meriting the least reward (Isa. 64:6; Rom. 3:23). Only grace, which is free and unmerited, brings the soul to glory. For heaven is purchased at no other price than that of the Redeemer's precious blood. His dying love and redeeming mercy are so unspeakable, so vastly great, that eternity will scarcely be sufficient to utter them.

Epenetus: Well, worthy Junius—

Junius: Do not call me worthy, for none is worthy here but He who sits upon the throne and the blessed Lamb of God. To ascribe all glory to Him is a great part of our happiness here, for there are myriads of saints and angels around the throne, continually crying with a loud, yet melodious voice, *"Worthy is the Lamb that was slain to receive power, and riches, and wisdom, and strength, and honour, and glory, and blessing"* (Rev. 5:12). No, no, my Epenetus, there is no crediting anything to creatures. Here those who wear the brightest crowns cast them before the throne, saying, "You are worthy, O Lord, to receive glory, honor, and power."

Epenetus: Dear Junius, bear with me a little because I am still weighed down with mortality. O that I were but once freed of it! O that I with you might see the great Three One and seeing, be transformed into His likeness, which as I have heard the blessed Elijah tell, is the completion of all happiness.

Junius: My dear Epenetus, the blessed vision is what does indeed complete our happiness. It fills our souls with love and joy, a fullness that is inexpressible and only known by those who feel it. But you must know, my Epenetus, the strongest and most enlarged faculties of all the bright intellects here can bear but little of those radiant beams of divine glory. They are so overwhelming, for there is no comparison between the grandest of created beings and the indescribable glory of the great Creator.

Epenetus: O noble Junius, I readily believe what you have said, but yet I think I am willing to know all I can of what I can never know enough of. And since I know there is nothing more delightful than to be always exercised in the displaying of the glory of the great Author of your happiness, deny not, dearest Junius, to your friend—for such you know I ever was and am—the satisfaction of hearing from your lips the mighty wonders of divinest love. Permit me to join with you to sing His praise. Display those mysteries of His providence, which to the world below are all dark, but to your now enlarged understanding are seen in their true light.

WHAT GOD HAS BLESSED US WITH

Junius: The praises of the Divine Majesty, O my dear Epenetus, will be the mighty subject of our song through all the ages of eternity. Both saints and angels join together and make up one great chorus. Therefore, what you have asked of me, I will gladly undertake so that you may see by what He has done that He alone is worthy of your love and of the praises we ascribe to Him. For the most ardent love of all the blessed saints and angels here is nothing else but the reflection of His love for us. He who lay on Love's own bosom told us, *"We love him, because he first loved us"* (1 John 4:19).

Therefore, my dear Epenetus, since the love of God for us is the foundation of our love for Him, let me present you first with an idea of His love for us and the advantages that we receive thereby. They are so many that they are past numbering; the mighty sum exceeds all arithmetic can count. But that I may, as you were intimating, set things in a true light, first I will show you how much we owe His love and goodness for all His free and undeserved favors granted to us in the world below.

All We Possess

Junius: First, in the world below, we owed to His goodness no less than all the goods we possessed. All that we were and all that we enjoyed were wholly owing to Him: *"It is he that hath made us, and not we ourselves"* (Ps. 100:3). We were in His hands like clay that is in the potter's (Isa. 64:8). He could have made us any other creatures. We were so opposite from that from which we were extracted. Had He so desired, He could have left us forever as that first nothing from which we had our being. Of necessity, then, His love is the first and original fountain of blessing. All other blessings are as conduit pipes through which He conveys His love to us. He who does not see God's love is blind.

Perhaps a man gets applause because of His wisdom, and through His diligence, He heaps up treasures. But was it not from God that man received wisdom? And did God not both give and prosper all man's boasted efforts? Surely God gave us all we enjoy as much as when someone gives a beggar a thousand pounds, and in so doing gives him food, clothing, and all that thousand pounds can help him to buy, which otherwise he would not have had.

Deliverance from Misery

Junius: Secondly, besides all these more obvious presents of His bounty, there are many things in the world below from which we were delivered. They enhance the value of His divine goodness to us. Although they are, perhaps, less conspicuous, they are no less prized by those below. The lack of them causes their true value to be recognized.

Should I, my Epenetus, lead your thoughts into the galleys and show you there those wretched captives who lie chained to their oars, exposed to all the miseries and hardships of a tempestuous sea? Yet because of the barbarous treatment they experience on shore, they fear the ocean less than any port, except death. Or should I draw back the curtains of the sick and dying and open to you that sad scene of sorrow in which so many pine and languish with diseases so very grievous to be endured that death is rather to be chosen than life? Or should I take you to the hospitals and show you there the various shapes of human miseries? If I were to show you all these things, would you not, my dear Epenetus, think it a mercy worthy of acknowledging to be delivered from them? Should we not prize that Divine Goodness who has thus made us different and freed us from those various sorts of miseries to which so many mortals are exposed?

Sometimes, His wisdom finds it necessary to exercise His own beloved children with long continued sickness, sharp pains, and other great calamities.

But this, my Epenetus, is still a further evidence of His love so that He might preserve them from the far worse contagion of their sins or cure them of the evil habits they had contracted.

Have you not seen, my Epenetus, in the world below, a tender mother apply a painful, burning medication to the neck of her beloved infant in an effort to make her child well? And have you not concluded that she thinks the trouble of an ulcer is a lesser evil than for her child to experience convulsions?

So when we see the ever blessed God, our heavenly Father, send infirmities and crosses to rescue those He loves from sin's dominion, we safely conclude that He thinks affliction is a far less evil than the guilt of sin. He is too wise and too indulgent a physician to cure with such a remedy as would be worse than the disease.

You may remember, Epenetus, that God through Moses gives the Israelites a caution, lest prosperity, which is so apt to make men forget everything but their enjoyments, should make any of them say in their hearts, *"My power and the might of mine hand hath gotten me this wealth"* (Deut. 8:17).

On the contrary, He commands them to remember the Lord their God, *"for it is he that giveth* [them] *power to get wealth"* (v. 18). And there was need enough of such a caution, for we are too apt to forget that God gave us our corn, our wine, and our oil.

His Love

Junius: Third, the Divine Goodness exceedingly recommends the advantageousness of His love to us. While we were below, He gave us so great a promise of spiritual goods and expected joys that it made even the pledge large enough to subsist upon with comfort. It really outweighed and far transcended all those momentary pleasures it required us to forsake in order to hold on to a title to eternal ones.

Although the mercies that the ever blessed God bestowed on us in the life below were both so many and so great as made it a fit theme to praise Him in heaven, His love is more lasting than anything in the world below. It does not, with our bodies or like the usual custom of our friends below, accompany us to our graves and leave us. No, Epenetus, God's love appears most bright when our dark eyes are closed. It cleaves closest to the soul when it forsakes the body, giving each blessed saint who arrives here good ground to say of Him what Naomi once said of Boaz: He has *"not left off his kindness to the living and to the dead"* (Ruth 2:20). Therefore, now indeed, said our great Savior's happy favorite, *"Are we the sons of God, and it doth not yet appear what we shall be: but we know that, when he shall appear, we shall be like him"* (1 John 3:2). That is now my present theme.

It is the love of God, the ever blessed God, my Epenetus, that gives us this admission to heaven. Heaven is the bright seat of so much happiness that we here scarcely count among our joys that heaven is the seat of them. As much emptiness as the world's pleasures contain, heaven's pleasures exceed our expectations of delight. For you have already heard the apostle who told us, *"Eye hath not seen, nor ear heard, neither have entered into the heart of man, the things which God hath prepared for them that love him"* (1 Cor. 2:9).

THE INDESCRIBABLE PLEASURES OF HEAVEN

Junius: And now, my Epenetus, our own experiences tell us so. Those pure refined delights that we enjoy not only surpass our senses but are sublime enough to transcend imagination. For whatever our minds formed below as the most perfect idea and the most abstracted notion of complete happiness, our own happy experiences here greatly exceed our expectations. Heaven is a soil whose fruitfulness is so confined to joy that even our disappointments and mistakes, when in the world below, do here contribute to our happiness. Our joy here, which is a gift of God, cannot be adequately described even in the Sacred Oracles. Our thoughts about what we enjoyed below are not only removed but exalted above whatever we could imagine there. Nor will you wonder, Epenetus, that it should be so, if you will but consider that here our faculties are not only gratified with suitable and acceptable objects but are so heightened and enlarged that our capacities are both increased and filled.

79

Beyond Imagination

Junius: In the world below, a child not yet released from the humble prison of the womb cannot have any idea of the delights that will be afforded him by the pleasing noises and the glittering objects that will present themselves to him after his birth. And the same child, while he continues in his youth, though he may look with delight on emblems finely drawn and painted, cannot imagine what pleasure the same objects will afford him when age and study will have ripened his intellect and made him capable of understanding the excellent moralities couched in those curious symbols.

Such a double advantage, Epenetus, among others, the admission into these sacred mansions brings to all those to whom that blessing is granted. For besides that set of objects, if I may so speak, so new and so peculiar to this place that their ideas could never once enter into the thoughts of the blessed before they were admitted here, besides this, our now enlarged capacities enable us, even in objects not altogether unknown to us before, to perceive things formerly undiscerned and derive from them both new and greater satisfaction and delight.

Exaggeration Necessary

Junius: Wonder not, my Epenetus, that in describing these glorious things I use expressions you have not been used to hearing since my bright theme is more above our praises than this blessed region is above the earth. Although my language may seem exaggerated and lofty, apparent hyperboles may well be used in the description of blessed happiness, which makes the greatest hyperboles but suitable ones.

The joys of heaven appear as the stars do to the world below. Because of their remoteness from the earth, they appear to be extremely little, but they are so vast that one less than the largest is much greater than the biggest object on earth, no, than the whole earth itself. Therefore, Epenetus, considering you are still clothed with mortality, I endeavor to give you an account of heavenly things by descriptions transcending what they appear to you so that I may thereby give you notions less inferior to what they truly are.

Desires Fulfilled

Junius: For here, my Epenetus, the blessed enjoy happiness enough to rectify all those mistaken notions we had formed of it to ourselves below. We are instructed here both how to name and rate all the joys that we possess, which are made up of the coming together of perfection and eternal true joys. We are made happy, unlike what philosophy pretends to do, not by the confinement, but by the fulfillment of our utmost desires, which neither fail in the choice of their objects nor miss in the enjoyment of them. They are unerringly just and infallibly accomplished.

In the Company of Saints

Junius: Here we not only see, but are made like those blessed saints we in the world below so much admired—those *"spirits of just men made perfect"* (Heb. 12:23), of which the Scriptures have told us. Here they are our constant and familiar company, into whose blessed society we are not only welcome, but increase it. Here likewise we behold those glorious spirits whose nature does invest them with so bright a luster that all of the disadvantage their disguises gave them when they appeared to us below would scarcely suffice to hinder us from making them the object of our adoration.

In the Presence of the Lamb

Junius: But above all, we here behold, my Epenetus, a sight worth dying for: the blessed Lamb of God, *"slain from the foundation of the world"* (Rev. 13:8). That glorious Savior, of whom the Scripture does so excellently present to us, has done and suffered so much for us. Both on account of His infinite perfection and His inestimable benefits, He highly deserves our praise.

Yes, Epenetus, here we behold that holy and divine Person, who, when He promised to pitch His tent among the sons of men below and dwell with them on the earth in order to fit them by His merits and example to dwell with Him in heaven, did in so admirable a manner mix an awesome majesty with a humble meekness and the assumed infirmities of His human nature with the brilliance of His divine. In His whole life, He expressed so perfect and exemplary a virtue, with so much sweetness and gentleness toward those who were aspirers to it, though they came most short of it, that even the Jews themselves could say of Him, *"He hath done all things well"* (Mark 7:37). Even more, His very enemies, who were employed to apprehend Him as a malefactor, confessed to those who sent them that *"never man spake like* [Him]*"* (John 7:46).

But there, my Epenetus, this blessed Son of God was in *"the form of a servant"* (Phil. 2:7), which He put on so that He might suffer for us and exercise His priestly and prophetic functions in the world below. But here, we see Him in that regal state and condition that belongs to Him by virtue of His kingly office, *"the King of kings, and Lord of lords"* (1 Tim. 6:15). All power and authority are invested in Him, both in heaven and earth (Matt. 28:18).

We Behold His Glory

Junius: He is encompassed with such radiant majesty and splendor that we may well judge Him to be the most admirable. For here our ravished souls, by an attentive contemplation of His glories, still find more cause to imitate the spouse in Solomon's mystic song, who having dwelt on the beauty of the several excellencies of the divine bridegroom breaks into this exclamation, *"He is altogether lovely!"* (Song 5:16).

His sparkling eyes appear in His exalted glory on the throne like flames of active fire. Into the ravished hearts of the beholders, they shoot flames as pure, as holy, and as deathless as what the seraphim themselves consist of.

Surely, Epenetus, since the Divine Oracles do assure us, as I have already said, it has never *"entered into the heart of man, the things which God hath prepared for them that love him"* (1 Cor. 2:9). That glory can be but imperfectly expressed. The blessed God rewards the meritorious sufferings and obedience of the only begotten Son of His love, for whose sake He is pleased to confer on all the numerous company of His elect such unimaginable glories. He who grants to so many of His servants a brightness like that of the stars, you cannot but think, Epenetus, does communicate a far more radiant luster to the Sun of Righteousness, although your present mortal state denies you to behold the brightness of His glory.

We Receive His Welcome

Junius: But all this glorious greatness of our blessed Redeemer does not make His kindness less familiar, but only more obliging. Even after His ascension, He does not disdain to say, *"Behold, I stand at the door, and knock: if any man hear my voice, and open the door, I will come in to him, and will sup with him, and he with me"* (Rev. 3:20). And that king in the parable, by whom our blessed Lord is represented, is pleased to welcome each individual trustworthy servant with a distinctive, *"Well done, thou good and faithful servant"* (Matt. 25:21).

Jesus Makes It Heaven

Junius: Wonder not, Epenetus, that I seem so solicitous to give you an account of the high dignity and supereminent joy of our exalted Savior and that I have endeavored thus to let you know that the bright Sun of Righteousness is now incapable of suffering eclipses but shines with an unclouded and unequaled splendor. Wonder not that I now see Jesus, who, as the author of the Hebrews speaks, was made a *"little lower than the angels,"* crowned *"with glory and honour"* (Heb. 2:7). For it makes heaven to be more heaven to me to find Him reigning here, who suffered so much for me in the world below.

And our Redeemer's happiness, which is so great and so indescribable, brings an increase to ours, according to the ardency of our love for Him. Let me add that though our joys are so great here, they do not need endearing circumstances; however, our Redeemer's happiness makes our happiness increase since it is more a proof of His love than a special gift of His bounty.

It was a matter of rejoicing to the disgraced apostles that they were *"counted worthy to suffer shame for his name"* (Acts 5:41). How much, do you think, is their joy now that they are admitted to reign with Him? Having supported the hardships and toils to which the afflicted condition of our mortality was exposed, He did so much alleviate them and refresh us under them that even in this sense it also might be truly said, *"The chastisement of our peace was upon him; and with his stripes we are healed"* (Isa. 53:5).

We Share the Master's Joy

Junius: But can you think, Epenetus, that He, who has redeemed us by His cross, does not do more for us by His crown? Here He not only admits but also invites each faithful servant to no less a blessing than to enter into His Master's joy. (See Matthew 25:21.) So rich a source of happiness did Christ make Himself to us in all His capacities and conditions that on earth and in heaven, it was and is His gracious and constant employment to share our griefs or to impart to us His joys. He either lessens our miseries by His sufferings or increases our happiness by His joy.

We See Our Friends and Family
Who Have Died in the Faith

Junius: Having thus examined the happiness of those celestial mansions resulting from the blessed sight of our redeeming Lord, the Crown of all our blessedness, I now proceed to tell you, Epenetus, what you perhaps may have observed already. Here we see not only our elder brother Christ, but also our friends, kindred, and relations, who in the world below lived in His fear and died in His favor. This fact is a large addition to our happiness.

We Know the Saints Who Went before Us

Junius: Not only do we know our friends, relations, and contemporaries but also all the saints who lived in all the ages of the world. Thus, though Elijah, whom I found conversing with you, lived in the world a long time before the blessed Messiah was made flesh, you no sooner saw him than you knew him, and you will do so with Adam when you see him.

Nor can I think this is a new notion to you since you might long ago have learned it from the Sacred Scriptures. Our blessed Savior Himself told us that the children of the Resurrection will be like the angels (Matt. 22:30), who in the visions both of the prophet Daniel and the apostle John appear to be acquainted with each other. Also, in the parable of the miserable rich man and the happy beggar, the father of the faithful is represented as knowing not only the person and present condition, but also the past story of Lazarus (Luke 16:19-25). Moreover, when in the world below, the Apostle of the Gentiles expected his converted and pious Thessalonians to be his crown at that great day (1 Thess. 2:19–20). Having turned many to righteousness, they will, as the beloved Daniel tells us, confer a starlike and immortal brightness (Dan. 12:3).

I am sure, my Epenetus, you have often read of the transfiguration of the blessed Redeemer in the holy mount where Moses and Elijah were talking with Him. You cannot forget how readily the three disciples knew them. This was no other but a type of heaven where all the saints are known to one another.

Do you think our knowledge here is less than what Adam had in his first state of innocence? Yet you know that Adam knew Eve his wife when she was first brought to him, and he told her that she was bone of his bone and flesh of his flesh (Gen. 2:23). But why would you need further examples? Your own experience has already told you that it is so. When you are divested of mortality, as in a little while you will be, you will find it with far greater evidence.

Perfect Unity

Junius: But let me show you, my dear Epenetus, the great advantage that the knowledge of each other here does bring to all the blessed.

Here the blessed dwell in an uninterrupted perfect union and communion with God and with each other. Without knowledge, there can be no agreement; without agreement, no communion; and without communion, there is no happiness. To think that we do not know each other here would be to think us short of happiness. Here, the *"general assembly...of the firstborn"* (Heb. 12:23), as they receive their happiness from the bright vision of the ever blessed God, in turn communicate the purest pleasure to each other, an unfeigned, ardent love uniting all that pure society.

Perfect Love

Junius: On earth, our love was kindled, either from some natural relation or other civil tie or on account of some visible excellencies that made a person worthy of our choice and friendship. But here, our reasons are far greater, and the degrees of love incomparably more fervent. In this supernatural state, all carnal alliances and respects do cease. The blessed apostle, even when on earth, told us that if he had known Christ *"after the flesh,"* he knew Him so no more (2 Cor. 5:16). For by the Resurrection and Ascension of our blessed Lord, he had been transported into another world and had had communion with Him as a heavenly king, without low regards to the temporal privilege of conversing with Him on earth.

Our spiritual relation is more near and permanent than the strictest bond of nature. Here we all have relation to the same heavenly Father and to Jesus Christ, the Prince of Peace, and Head of our happy fraternity. The principal motives of love, even on earth, are the inherent characteristics of a person. Wisdom, holiness, goodness, and fidelity are mighty attractions to affection and produce a more intimate confederacy of souls than kinship in nature or any other carnal respects.

Virtue is admirable in an elderly person, though he is wrinkled and deformed, and vice is hateful in a young person, though she is beautiful. And you have seen on earth, my Epenetus, clearer eyes than those of flesh, a purer light than what is sensible, a diviner beauty than what is fleshly, and a nobler love than what is sensual, which made the royal prophet declare that all his delight was in the excellent (Ps. 16:3).

But even spiritual love has its impurities below. For there are relics of frailty in the best of men and some blemishes that make them less likable. But here, the image of God is complete by the union of all the glorious virtues necessary for its perfection. Every blessed soul agrees exactly with the first Exemplar. A divine beauty shines in them, ever durable. It is a beauty that emits no contagious fires, a beauty that is inviolable and cannot suffer injury.

The true worth of the saints below is not very visible; only the least part of it is seen. The earth is fruitful in its plants and flowers, but its riches are in mines of precious metal and veins of marble hidden in its bosom. On earth, true grace appears in sensible actions, but its glory is within. Here the excellencies of the blessed are in open view. The glory of the blessed God is revealed in them, and how attractive is the divine likeness to a holy eye. I am overcome to see my fellow saints shining with an immortal loveliness!

Their love is reciprocal, proportional to the cause of it. An equal, constant flame is preserved by pure materials. Here every one is perfectly amiable and perfectly enamored of each other. How happy is this state of love! Well might the psalmist break forth with that rapturous note, *"Behold, how good and how pleasant it is for brethren to dwell together in unity!"* (Ps. 133:1), had he then seen that happy union that he now here enjoys with all the faithful ones.

Love is the beauty and the strength of all societies and the great pleasure of our lives below. How excellent then must the joy be of the blessed here who witness the accomplishment of what our Savior prayed for when on earth: *"That they may be one, even as we are one: I in them, and thou in me, that they may be made perfect in one"* (John 17:22).

The blessed God is absolutely one in His glorious nature and will; therefore, He is unalterably happy. The inviolable unity of the saints' love is a bright ray of the essential unity among the sacred persons. Here love effectively transforms one soul into another and makes the glory of each saint overflow to the joy of all. Such is the power of this celestial fire. Where we burn, it melts and mines souls in such an entire union that by complaisance and an intimate joy, the blessedness of all is, as it were, proper to everyone, as if everyone were placed in the hearts of all and all in the heart of everyone.

Perfect Friendship

Junius: And where there is love like this, all needs must be delight. How can it be otherwise since in this blessed society there is a continual receiving and returning of love and joy, with mutual reciprocations of endearment. Their conversation and communion is enchanting. Think, Epenetus, what all entertainment of love and joy there is in the presence and conversations of dear friends below. How their shared viewpoints, like a chain composed of bright spirits, fasten and draw their souls to one another! And though there are no friendships on the earth without imperfections, the felicity of love consists in their conversation.

Whatever is commendable in friendship is in perfection here; whatever is imperfect, occasioned by men's folly or their weakness, is abolished here. With overflowing of affection, the blessed here recount the divine benefits and all those admirable methods whereby the life of grace was first begun, preserved, and carried on amid temptations, the succession of mercies in the time of our hopes, and the consummation of all in this time of our enjoyment.

United Praise

Junius: Have you not yet heard, Epenetus, the melody that both saints and angels make about the throne? And how they all concur in their thanksgivings to God for making them reasonable creatures, such as are capable both of loving and enjoying Him when they might have been of the lowest order in the whole sphere of beings; for His compassionate care and providence over them in the world; but especially for His sovereign and singular mercy in electing them to be vessels of honor; for His powerful grace, in rescuing them from the cruel and ignominious bondage of sin; and for His free love that justified them from all their guilt by the death of His only Son and has now glorified them with Himself.

We are never weary, Epenetus, of this delightful exercise but continually bless Him for His mercy that endures forever. Yes, the winged cherubim and seraphim about the throne cry one to another to express their zeal and joy in celebrating His eternal purity and power and the glory of His goodness. How unspeakable is the pleasure of this concert! Every soul is harmonious and contributes its part to the full music of heaven. Could the world below but hear the echo of those songs with which the heavens above resound, those songs of triumph of the saints justly praising and solemnly adoring the King of spirits, how it would inflame their desires to be joined with them!

The Mysteries of Scripture Are Revealed

Junius: Besides all the happiness that accumulates to us by the knowledge of our friends, kindred, and relations and what results from the communion we have with God and with each other, it is to me, my Epenetus, a mighty happiness I enjoy from understanding satisfactorily all those deep and obscure mysteries of religion. The most profound rabbis of the world below were not ashamed to admit they could not fully comprehend some passages that they admire but can never fathom. It is a mighty pleasure that here I understand those passages of the Sacred Scriptures that all the bold critics and learned expositors have attempted to illustrate. Yet to the world below, they remain obscure. It cannot be otherwise because they cannot discern how exquisitely the several parts of Scripture are fitted to the various times, persons, and occurrences wherein their omniscient Author intended to use them the most. All are obvious to us here; consequently, we discern a perfect harmony between those texts that in the world below seemed to be in conflict.

Here, Epenetus, we have clearly expounded to us those riddles of providence, which have often tempted even good men on earth to question God's conduct in the government of the world. While calamities and persecutions of virtue and innocence seem approved by Him, it appears that He heaps prosperity on their criminal opposers. Here we are thoroughly convinced that all those seeming irregularities, which the heathen thought fit to impute to the giddy whimsies of a female deity, are not only consistent with divine justice and goodness, but are productions of it. What intelligent persons in the world below find difficult to understand, here are revealed to be reasonable.

Bildad, who was one of Job's well-meaning but unkind comforters, told us long ago that they who live on the earth *are but of yesterday, and know nothing"* (Job 8:9). Their days there are but a shadow (v. 9); the shortness of their transitory lives does not permit them to continue long enough as spectators to see more than a scene or two at the most of that great play acted by humankind on the stage of the world. It is no wonder that they are apt to harbor sinister thoughts against the Contriver of the plot. They are acquainted with neither the beginning nor the end.

But once the whole of divine conduct in the administration of things will be disclosed, as here it is, all those revolutions and occurrences of empires, states, families, and particular persons, which mortals are so prone to quarrel with below, do here to us appear to be so just, so necessary, so timely. Those very things that while we were on earth tempted us to deny God, here engage us to praise Him. Indeed, we are not so properly satisfied, as seized, with the beauty of His providence.

THE REASON FOR EARTHLY TRIALS

Junius: Besides this general providence of God and His loving wisdom, here we are especially transported with wonder and gratitude at those discoveries of the divine goodness. He kindly reveals the reasons for His favors toward each one in particular. O Epenetus, I have seen for myself not only the necessity and justice, but even the mercy, of those very afflictions that I once, when on the earth, credited to His severity.

I am now fully convinced that no blows I met with in the world below, and you know, my Epenetus, that there I met with many great afflictions, either came sooner, fell heavier, or lasted longer than the occasion demanded. I am satisfied my hopes were never disappointed but that they secured my title to better things than what I hoped for. Nor was my welfare ever injured, but instead, things were working to my advantage. (See Romans 8:28.)

Yes, Epenetus, all that unwelcome darkness, which on earth surrounded my blind understanding is now vanished. It did so at the first dawning of this bright eternal day. The resolution of all those difficulties, which on the earth not only exercised but distressed my faith, is granted to reward it.

THE BLESSED ENJOY THE FELLOWSHIP OF GOD

Junius: Here, Epenetus, to draw to a conclusion, we do not only converse with saints and angels, but with that far more infinitely glorious Deity who made them what they are without at all depleting Himself. Here we not only enjoy heaven, but its Maker, God. We see Him as He is, who is our all in all, comprising all the good we value in the creatures more eminently and fully than the bright luminary of the day excels the twinkling tapers of the night.

For we are so taken with the contemplation and enjoyment of that glorious One in whose infinity all good is both included and enlarged that ages numberless, as are the joys the blissful vision does abound with, will scarcely afford us leisure for a diversion to any other pleasures than those His presence creates, which are so numerous and so entire. We desire nothing that we do not have except more tongues to sing more praises to the blessed God or a capacity to pay Him greater thanks for what we have.

The Blessed Experience Perfect Happiness

Junius: The residents of these bright mansions scarcely know any other need than the need to wish. The complete blessedness of our condition reduces us to a happy usefulness of wishes by giving us so full a prior possession of all the objects of desire. Time, like fire that destroys whatever it preys on, at last dies itself and so goes out into eternity. The nature of our joy is such that though after some centuries it may seem to grow older because of having been enjoyed so many ages, it really continues as welcome and as fresh as at the first. It is the unique property of our happiness: it is always the same, yet ever new. Weariness argues imperfection either in the object or the appetite; the former is impossible in God, and the latter ceases here.

The Joy of the Blessed Is Ever Fresh

Junius: For our blessedness here is so great, there is no need for variety to be a part of it. If it does admit variety, it is such a one as consists only in the continued knowledge of its first object, God. It is like what may be seen on earth in the diversified refractions of the same sparkling diamond. In God, there is, if I may properly speak, such an identical variety that the enjoyment of Him both satisfies and creates desires that are without complete fullness and yet without distress.

Other delights do, like the clothes men wear, grow old and quickly wear out; however, those heavenly pleasures we enjoy share in that characteristic of the garments of the Israelites in the wilderness, which were not impaired by being used long.

As the needle once touched with a magnet would never, uncompelled, forsake it, but after ages clings no less closely to it than at the first moment of their union, so do the blessed here, with the same undiminished freshness, ever possess their joys, as if each moment were the first that they possessed them.

If our happiness does not improve by our enjoyment of it, it is perhaps because the greatness of it makes it incapable of increasing. Or if our pleasures do increase, it is from our assurance that we will taste them forever and perpetually repeat the same renewed enjoyment for all eternity. They become more valuable as in quiet leisure, we celebrate Jehovah's praises without distraction. We are past suffering ill.

In brief, our inexhausted joys are here so numberless and so immense that we will need, as well as have, eternity itself to taste them fully.

THE JOY OF THE BLESSED IS IMMEASURABLE

Junius: But I remember, Epenetus, you still are in the body and may be tired of hearing what I could be forever relating. So vast is the happiness that I possess and so great is the pleasure in relating it. Therefore, I will now add only one property of our enjoyed happiness. The vast multitude of blessed souls who are partakers of this joy and glory detracts nothing from each private share, nor lessens the property each happy saint has in it in particular. This ocean of joy is so bottomless that the innumerable company of all the saints and angels never can exhaust it.

Nor is this strange at all, for in the world below, which does consist of many spacious countries and many of them divided from one another by large seas, each nation alike enjoys the benefit of light. None can complain that they enjoy it less because another enjoys it too, but all enjoy its benefit as fully as if no one else enjoyed it but themselves. Indeed, there is this difference between the Sun of Righteousness and what shines on the world below. By its presence, the latter eclipses all the planets. The former, though radiant with a much greater splendor, will by His presence impart it to His saints as the great Apostle of the Gentiles informs you where he said, *"When Christ, who is our life, shall appear, then shall ye also appear with him in glory"* (Col. 3:4).

This is the language of each blessed soul to his Redeemer: *"I am my beloved's, and my beloved is mine"* (Song 6:3). For each has a special claim to Him. And David, so well skilled in singing songs of praise to his Redeemer, says of all those who put their trust in God that He will abundantly satisfy them with the fatness of His house and make them drink of the river of His pleasures (Ps. 36:7–8). It is as if he meant to make comparisons. When a multitude of persons drink of the same river, none of them is able to exhaust it, yet each of them has the full liberty of drinking as much as he can, or as much as he could, as though none but himself should be allowed to drink of it. In the same way, whoever enjoys God enjoys Him wholly or at least enjoys Him so entirely in relation to his capacity that the enjoyment of whatever rests unenjoyed in God is forgiven by the immensity of the object and not the prior possession of his companions.

Thus, Epenetus, I have given you a brief account of our celestial Canaan. It is not indeed the thousandth part of what might be said, yet it is enough to let you see it is a land flowing with milk and honey. It may well serve to whet your longing for a more fruitful and experiential knowledge of it. No one can fully know the happiness we enjoy here until he comes to be a partaker of it.

Junius finished his excellent discourse, and I thanked him repeatedly. I assured him that I was not tired in the least from hearing what he had to say; instead, I was exceedingly delighted as well as informed by it. I could not be more pleased in hearing a description of that happiness, which through the abundant merits of my blessed Redeemer, I hoped in a short time to be a partaker of.

Junius: To wait with *"faith and patience"* (Heb. 6:12) until your mortal body is laid down is what is now your work. Then you will know far more than I have told you. You will hear, see, and know things then after another quantity than you now do. Your ears are not yet fitted to hear those melodies that saints and angels sing before the throne, nor can your tongue repeat those songs of praise, which here the blessed make continually. Your eyes, though strengthened above those of other mortals, cannot yet behold the brightness of the glory that fills this happy place, though I must grant what you have seen has given you more suitable ideas of it than all who live below can make of heavenly things. This is a favor so great and inexpressible that you have mighty cause to magnify His great, exceeding grace through whose abundant goodness you were admitted here.

EPENETUS ASKS TO SEE HIS MOTHER

Epenetus: That blessed work cannot begin too soon, and it is a work I hope will never end but be as lasting as the cause of it. But, Junius, since I have had the happiness of this conversation with you, may I not also see my mother here? I am sure she is among the blessed. In my early years, she instructed me every day to read the holy Scriptures. Her pious exhortations first of all made me look after heavenly and eternal things, and on her dying bed, she gave me a charge that whatever others did, I should serve the Lord. I am sure she would rejoice to see me in this place.

IN HEAVEN, EARTHLY RELATIONSHIPS CEASE

Junius: Your mother, Epenetus, is here indeed and will, no doubt, rejoice in God on your account as she continually does on her own, but in this happy place, worldly relations cease. There is neither male nor female here. All are like the angels (Matt. 22:30), for souls cannot be distinguished into sexes; therefore, all relations here are swallowed up in God. However, you will presently see she whom you called mother in the world below.

He had no sooner spoken than he took me by the hand. Far swifter than an arrow from a bow, we passed by several shining forms, clothed in robes of immortality. They seemed to wonder at me as I passed them. I thought it was occasioned by my being there in the poor rags of frail mortality. Junius, having brought me to my mother, for so I still thought of her though she now appeared as a shining form, addressed me one last time.

JUNIUS DEPARTS

Junius: Farewell, my Epenetus, I have now done what you have desired of me. Your guardian angel will be with you right away and guide you to the world below. When you arrive there, do not cease to celebrate the mighty wonders of Divine Love, who has so far indulged your weakness as to admit you here and allowed you with earthly eyes to see the immaterial glories of the blessed.

EPENETUS IS REUNITED WITH HIS MOTHER

The noble Junius having left me, I immediately drew near to the shining form that stood before me. She was surrounded with rays of dazzling luster and appeared extremely glorious. I could hardly behold her for the exceeding brightness of her countenance. I looked with more intenseness on her than on Elijah or the noble Junius. But taking it for granted it was my mother, I thus addressed her.

Epenetus: My dearest mother, I joy to see you clothed in that bright robe of glory as an inhabitant of these blessed realms of light and immortality.

TESTIMONY TO GOD'S FAITHFULNESS

Mother: Dear Epenetus, for what I am, to Him who is on the throne and to the Lamb be all the praise and glory, for He alone has made me so. This robe of glory, which you see me wear, is only the reflection of His own bright beams! Ah, Epenetus, had not the blessed, forever blessed redeeming Jesus, first clothed me with His robe of righteousness, I

103

never would have worn this robe of glory. I do not ask you, Epenetus, how you come to be admitted here, for I have had a full account of that already from Elijah and must acknowledge that the Divine Condescension has been exceeding great in this permission. Eternal praise be given to Him.

Epenetus, through how many dangers divine grace conducts our souls to glory! I cannot think, but with the most admiring thoughts of Divine Love, how near I was to eternal ruin. Once I was poor, blind, and naked (see Revelation 3:17), cast out into the loathing of my person and polluted in my filth and blood. O the abundant grace that found me in that wretched, sad condition, and yet to me made it a time of love! He washed me from all my filthiness and purged me from my sin! I once was nothing else but darkness, but, O miraculous and happy change, now I am full of light, love, and joy.

I once was poor and miserable, but now I am enriched with all that heaven can give or I can receive. Once I was naked and exposed to shame, but now I am adorned with robes of light and glory. I once was under sentence of eternal separation from the divine presence, but now I am possessed of God, my only Life and Joy and Supreme Good. How transporting is the comparison of these contrary extremes! How pleasant is the bright day of eternity after a night so dark and so tempestuous! How a vivid sense of those past evils produces a far more lively feeling and enjoyment of my happiness! This makes the everlasting hallelujahs that I sing to my

victorious Deliverer more ravishing and more harmonious.

I must confess I was amazed to find my mother
in such an ecstasy and holy transport. I could not
help responding.

Epenetus: Ah, my dear mother, you speak like
one who is indeed in heaven, and I feel the mighty
joys you possess.

Mother: O Epenetus, you should not think this
strange. The mighty wonders of divine love and
grace will be the subject of our songs forever. Nor
should you call me mother here, although I once was
so. Here all such relations cease, and are all swallowed up in God, who alone is the great Father of all
this heavenly family.

I must tell you, Epenetus, you are far dearer to
me as one who loves and fears the Lord than as the
son born of my body. Through faith, you are His
adopted son. Here it is our greatest mercy that we
have God as the Fountain of our happiness. All that
we enjoy is in and through Him who is in every way
so adequate to all our most enlarged capacities. In
enjoying Him, we enjoy all that we can ask or think.
(See Ephesians 3:20.)

I then desired to know if I should tell her in
what condition I left my father and my brothers in
the world below when I was carried here.

Mother: No, since I have put off the body, I have also laid aside all relations in the flesh. Here God is all to me. I have no husband but the blessed Bridegroom of my soul. He is fairer than the children of men and alone is desirable to me, nor do I have any other relations here. We are all children of one Father and servants of one Master, whose blessed service is our perfect freedom.

As for those I left behind in the world below, I have committed them to God in whose good pleasure I am happy. I will be glad and heartily rejoice to see them all heirs of this blessed inheritance, for then I will be well assured the will of God is so. But if they should join in with the grand Enemy of their salvation, refuse the grace that is offered them, and thereby perish in their unbelief, God will be glorified in His justice. In His glory, I will still rejoice. But since, dear Epenetus, you must descend again into the world below, you cannot better show your love for God and zeal for the promoting of His glory than by endeavoring to turn them to the ways of righteousness. Nor do you know but that might be one reason why this distinctive privilege has been allowed to you.

THE MARTYRED GLORIFY GOD

While I was thus conversing with my mother, a numerous company passed before me, clothed in long robes white as the morning's brightness and far purer than anything that ever yet deserved that name, having crowns of glory on their heads, which sparkled forth radiant in luster. Each one carried a palm of victory in his right hand. As they passed by, I heard them say, *"Salvation to our God which sitteth upon the throne, and unto the Lamb"* (Rev. 7:10). Another company whom I took to be angels had a very glorious appearance and covered their faces with their wings. They answered them, by saying, *"Amen: Blessing, and glory, and wisdom, and thanksgiving, and honour, and power, and might, be unto our God for ever and ever. Amen"* (v. 12).

I then inquired who that great company was, who were arrayed in garments of so pure a white with palms of victory in their hands. I was told that they were the noble company of martyrs, who having endured great tribulations in the world and laid down their lives for the Word of God and the testimony that they held, now had their robes washed in the blood of the Lamb and had palms in their hands as tokens of victory (Rev. 7:9, 13–14). I then asked from where they came? I was answered that they came from under the altar, where they had been crying, *"How long, O Lord, holy and true, dost thou not judge and avenge our blood on them that dwell on the earth?"* (Rev. 6:10).

Epenetus: I thought that all the saints here had rest and peace and joy in God, which did not permit them to have any thoughts of revenge toward their fellow creatures. I was even more inclined to think so because many of them had prayed for their persecutors in the world below, even at the very stakes and when they had been under the hands of the executioners. It seems strange to me that their meek and forgiving spirits should be altered here in heaven.

Mother: The saints here do indeed possess rest and peace and joy in God, which is the sum of all their happiness, but having resigned themselves entirely to the divine good pleasure, they cannot but desire that God's will may be fulfilled in all respects. Therefore, knowing that it is the will of God to render tribulation to those who have troubled them, and that He designs to glorify Himself by bringing down His judgments on the anti-Christian whore, who has made herself drunk with the blood of the saints and of the martyrs of Jesus (Rev. 17:6), they cannot but desire the will of God to be done and that His name may be glorified. They know this will be the result of His executing judgment on the great whore. For when Babylon is fallen, a new song will be put into their mouths. Then it will be said, *"Rejoice over her, thou heaven, and ye holy apostles and prophets; for God hath avenged you on her"* (Rev. 18:20). Yea, then they will sing,

Alleluia; salvation, and glory, and honour, and power, unto the Lord our God: for true and righteous are his judgments: for he hath judged the great whore, which did corrupt the

earth with her fornication, and hath avenged
the blood of his servants at her hand.

(Rev. 19:1–2)

Therefore, praise our God, all you servants and you who fear His name both small and great. Again the saints sing hallelujah. So then their crying under the altar, *"How long, O Lord, holy and true, dost thou not judge and avenge our blood on them that dwell on the earth?"* (Rev. 6:10), is not out of any desire of revenge, but that God may be glorified for His righteous judgments.

ARE THE BLESSED AWARE OF EARTHLY HAPPENINGS?

Having declared my satisfaction in her answer, I desired to know whether the souls of the blessed understood what affairs were transacting in the world below and whether they had any concern therein.

Mother: The sum of all our knowledge here is to know God, the Fountain of all our happiness. As to the affairs of particular persons, we are not concerned with them and are ignorant of them. Although glorified creatures, we are still finite. Being present in all places is an attribute unique to God alone, to whose sight every creature is manifest.

The prosperity or adversity of the church below is described to us by the angels, who are ministering spirits sent forth to assist those who will be heirs of salvation (Heb. 1:14). From what we learn from them, we are excited to renew our praises to Him who sits upon the throne and to the Lamb forever. The admirable providences of God in the deliverance and preservation of His church are what we reflect on with the greatest pleasure and delight. We praise God with the greatest ardency of affection, desiring also that His glory and His people's happiness may be perfected by the redemption of the whole church, which will not be until the bride has made herself ready and the mystical body of Christ is completed.

HOW THE BLESSED SPEND THEIR TIME IN HEAVEN

I then told her I would ask her only one more thing, for I believed my guide was ready to come for me. I asked in what manner their time was spent in this blessed place, and what their general conversation was.

Mother: O my Epenetus, how much does that weight of mortality you still bear about you cloud your understanding even in these bright regions? You speak of us as still clothed with mortal flesh and consider not that here mortality is *"swallowed up of life"* (2 Cor. 5:4). Time is changed into eternity without succession or end. It is true that in the world below, there is a continual flux of time, which is divided into hours, days, weeks, months, and years, but here there is no such thing. There is no night by which days are distinguished or circling orbs that divide the several seasons of the year. One eternal, undivided point lasts forever here; therefore, Epenetus, there is no time to spend here.

THE CONVERSATION OF THE BLESSED

Mother: As to the other part of your question, what our general conversation with each other is, eternity can only fully answer. We all have work enough to do throughout the numerous ages of eternity. It is so very pleasant and delightful that it both creates our joy while increasing it. What is more delightful to the soul than knowledge? And you may then soon think how vast a field we have to explore it in. And as our knowledge increases, so do the adorations we pay to the Divine Author of it, for this is our particular happiness, that all our discussions here, of whatever kind, tend to illustrate the high praises and adoration of the indescribable Three One.

How many wonders of God, my Epenetus, shine forth in the works of nature in the world below, which still are hidden and undiscovered by the most elaborate inquirers into them? How many things are there below that you do not know how they are done, yet you are well assured that they are? Who can tell how a tree grows from a seed, or a variegated, carefully designed flower sprouts from a poor simple slip without any diversity? And yet that it does so is evident enough.

Why the magnetic stone attracts needles and amber picks up straws are two of the mysteries of nature that continue to puzzle the wisest of mortals. It is difficult to explain the secret details as to how they came to pass even though the matter of fact is very obvious. These things are made intelligible here, and all their secret causes are laid open to our view, which likewise excites our humblest adorations and renews praises to Him who is so *"excellent in working"* (Isa. 28:29).

Then again, the wondrous magnitude as well as formations of the celestial orbs, which vain astrologers pretend to understand both in their causes and effects, are here made known to the blessed, who being filled with highest admiration adore the ever blessed God for all His works of wonder.

Not that we have this knowledge barely by simple intuition, but by the mutual exercise of our analytic faculties, whereby our knowledge still becomes progressive. Nor do I deny but that by intuition, our here enlarged faculties receive a great addition, for here, at one view, we can behold more than we can successively below in many years, to which the swiftness of our motion also contributes.

But further yet, the works of God's almighty providence and with what wondrous wisdom He has overruled and governed all events are such themes as well become us here to be continually contemplating. The more we view, the more we find occasion still to magnify the great and glorious name of the great Author of our happiness.

These contemplations, Epenetus, were often exceedingly delightful to me when in the world below, where I saw things but very darkly and lost much of the beauty of them because of the vanity that was on my blind understanding. It prevented me from seeing what was far off. But now that all my intellectual faculties are both enlarged and perfected and I can see the whole of what I then had but a short and imperfect view, how much more pleasant and delightful it is. How much more must it magnify the wisdom of the Great Contriver to see men eager in the pursuit of their own designs and the fulfilling of their lusts. They do not have regard for anything besides self-gratification.

Yet to see how all these things are overruled by the divine good pleasure, bringing things long since decreed to pass although those instruments knew nothing of it, is indeed well-befitting Him who is so *"wonderful in counsel, and excellent in working"* (Isa. 28:29). To whom be glory and blessing and praise through all the endless ages of eternity.

The eternal Father had decreed our great Redeemer should be born in Bethlehem, for so the prophet Micah declared, saying,

> *But thou, Bethlehem Ephratah, though thou be little among the thousands of Judah, yet out of thee shall he come forth unto me that is to be ruler in Israel; whose goings forth have been from of old, from everlasting.* (Mic. 5:2)

But when the time drew near that He should be born, the Blessed Virgin lived at Nazareth with her espoused husband, Joseph. She planned nothing else but to wait there for the birth of the child, which would have contradicted what the prophet Micah by divine inspiration had long ago foretold.

Therefore, at this time, Augustus Caesar, the Roman emperor, sent out a decree that all the Empire should be taxed, and that each one, both men and women, must return to the city from which he or she had descended. This caused the blessed virgin and her espoused husband to go to Bethlehem (big as she was, and far was the way) so that they might be taxed there according to what Caesar had decreed. (See Luke 2:1–5.) There the Lord of Life must be born, according to what Micah prophesied. Caesar aimed only at getting his money. Yet that aim of his, through divine wisdom overruling it, was made a means to bring about the fulfilling of the prophecy in so important a matter as the birth of the Messiah. This tends exceedingly to magnify the mighty wisdom and overruling providence of God, who governs all events to His own glory and His people's good.

THE PROVIDENCE OF GOD REVEALED

Mother: You knew a person, Epenetus, in the world below who planned to go see a friend and stay at his house for a few days. As he was getting up on horseback, he fell down and broke his leg, which put a stop to his intended journey. This he considered to be a very great trial, but in a few days, he learned that his friend's house had burned down the very night he intended to have stayed there. All who were in the house that night died. This made him look on what he at first thought to be a catastrophe to be a mercy to him: the breaking of his leg was but in order to save his life. Many such instances of divine love and goodness might be given, which here the blessed retain a lively sense of and mention in their songs of praise and hallelujahs to God and to the Lamb.

Again, my Epenetus, here all the blessed are eternally employed in singing praises to Him who by His wondrous grace has brought them to His glory. Here we see plainly that gulf of everlasting ruin, in which we were so likely to plunge ourselves had He not stopped our way. He often hedged up our way with thorns so that we might not travel to destruction. The various methods of His grace, whereby He brought us to Himself, we here repeat one to another and join in one great chorus to His praise. While we praise Him, He streams forth beams of His grace on us, whereby we are assimilated more into His likeness, which is our highest happiness.

Thus, Epenetus, I have answered your last question, which you will better understand when you come to be clothed with immortality. In the meantime, *"walk worthy"* (Eph. 4:1) of the grace you have received. Do not let your achievements puff you up, but give to God the glory of His grace. Let what you have seen and heard have this effect: to make you so much more abhor yourself for your own vileness.

The great Apostle of the Gentiles, who, like yourself, was once admitted here, declares he soon met with a *"thorn in the flesh,"* lest he should have been puffed up too much by the abundant revelations that he had received (2 Cor. 12:7). Let his example, therefore, keep you humble. Humility will be your best defense. Such God exalts, while the proud He abases.

MOTHER DEPARTS

Mother: I see your guardian angel coming toward you; therefore, Epenetus, I will bid you farewell until you return. Then we will part no more.

She had no sooner spoken than she departed. The bright form that brought me from the world below into this place of happiness was present with me. I bowed to him.

Angel: Bow to the throne and not to me. I have already told you, I am your fellow creature. Therefore, worship God alone, for He alone is worthy of adoration. Have you observed those heavenly mansions well?

Epenetus: I have observed and have almost been ravished with their glory, but even here I could but see in part. Their splendor was too bright and too ethereal for my viewing. And yet the sight was so extremely delightful that I wish I could stay here forever.

Angel: I have a command to guide you to the world below. I am not only to return you to the earth from where I took you but first to lead you to the regions of the Prince of Darkness. There you may see the reward of sin and what incensed justice has prepared as the just judgment of the rebellion of those who would exalt themselves above the throne of the Most High.

But do not be afraid, for as I have an order to take you there, likewise I am to bring you back again and leave you in the world from where I took you until you have put off mortality. Then I will once more be your guide here where you will live forever with all the blessed.

These last words of the angel did, as it were, put new life into me, for to leave heaven for earth extremely disturbed me and would have made me inconsolable except that I knew the divine will was such. But to leave heaven for hell was what turned my very heart within me.

However, when I knew that it was the divine good pleasure that I should be returned from there to earth again, and that after I had put off mortality, I should then be reconducted up to heaven, I was a little comforted. I found within myself an entire resignation to the will of God; therefore, I spoke with some assurance to my guide.

Epenetus: What the blessed God has ordered, I will always be willing to obey. His great mercy I have already experienced so largely. Even in hell itself I will not fear if I but have His presence with me there.

117

Angel: Wherever the blessed God promises His presence, there is heaven, and while we are in hell, He will be with us.

HAS GOD MADE OTHER WORLDS?

Then bowing low before the Almighty's throne, swifter than thought, my guardian angel carried me ten thousand leagues below the celestial heavens. When I saw those mighty globes of fire, those ever burning lamps of the ethereal heavens, I thus addressed my bright conductor. I told him that I had heard when I was on the earth that each one of those fixed stars were worlds. I believed they might be because though here they are of such a mighty magnitude, they seem to us on earth such small things like what the earth seems here, although indeed the earth seems here more dark than they do to those who are on the earth. But having such an opportunity, I would willingly be informed of the truth.

Angel: To Him who is almighty, there is nothing impossible. Nor can there be a boundary set to infinity. The ever blessed God took six days' time to make the world below, but He could as well have made it in one moment if He had so determined. It was the putting forth of His almighty power that caused it. What that power can do, there is none who can tell except He who possesses it.

But to argue that just because He has the power to do it, then it is His will to do it is not good logic in the school of heaven. He does whatever He pleases, both in heaven above and in the earth below. What He pleases to reveal to us we know, and what He has not so revealed are secrets locked up in His own eternal counsel. It is a bold and presumptuous curiosity for any creature to inquire into them. There is no doubt but He can make as many worlds as there are stars in the heaven if it pleases Him, but that He has done so, He has not yet revealed, nor is it therefore our duty to inquire.

ON THE OUTSKIRTS OF HELL

By this time we had arrived at the lowest regions of the air where I saw multitudes of horrid forms and dismal dark appearances fly from the shining presence of my bright guide.

Epenetus: Surely, these are some of the troops of hell, so black and so frightening are their forms.

Angel: These are some of the apostate spirits who wander up and down in the air and on the earth like roaring lions seeking whom they may devour (1 Pet. 5:8). Though they are fled away from here, you will see them quickly in their own dark territories, for we are now on the borders of the infernal pit.

5

Visions of Hell and of the Torments of the Damned

I quickly found the words of my guide to be true, for we were soon surrounded with a darkness much blacker than night. It was attended with a stench more suffocating by far than that of burning brimstone. Likewise, my ears were filled with the horrid yellings of the damned spirits. In comparison to this, all the most discordant notes on earth were melodious music.

Angel: Now, you are on the verge of hell. Do not fear the power of the Destroyer, for my commission from the Imperial throne secures you from all dangers. Here you may hear from devils and damned souls the cursed causes of their endless ruin. What you have a mind to ask, inquire, and they will answer you. The devils cannot hurt you, though they would if they could, for they are bound by Him who has commissioned me. Because they perceive sensations, it makes them rage, fret, roar, and bite their hated chains, but all in vain.

LUCIFER ON HIS THRONE

Now we were within hell's territories, placed in the caverns of the infernal deep. There, where earth's center adjusts all things, all effects do in their causes sleep. In a sulfurous lake of liquid fire, bound with the unyielding chain of heaven's fixed decree, sat Lucifer upon a burning throne. His horrid eyes sparkled with hellish fury, as full of rage as his strong pains could make him. Those wandering fiends, which as we came from heaven fled before us, had given notice of our coming. All hell was in an uproar, which made Lucifer vent his horrid blasphemies against the blessed God. He spoke with such an air of arrogance and pride that it was clear he wanted only power, not rage or malice.

Lucifer: What does the Thunderer want? He already has my heaven and the radiant scepter my hand should bear. He confines me here in this dark house of death, sorrow, and woe, far from those never fading fields of light, my fair inheritance. What! Would He have hell from me too that He insults me here? Could I obtain another day to try it in, I would make heaven shake and His bright throne totter. Nor would I fear the utmost of His power even if He had fiercer flames than these to throw me into. Though I lost the day then, the fault was not mine. No winged spirit in heaven's arched roof bid fairer for the victory than I did. But, oh, that day is lost, and I am doomed, forever doomed, to these dark territories! But it is at least some comfort to me still that mankind's sorrow waits on my woe. And since I cannot inflict the utmost of my rage on the Thunderer, I will inflict it on them.

I was amazed to hear his irreverent speech and could not keep from saying to my guide, "How justly his blasphemies are rewarded!"

Angel: What you have heard from this apostate spirit is both his sin and punishment, for every blasphemy he belches against heaven makes hell the hotter to him.

CONVERSATION OF THE DAMNED

We then passed on farther among dismal scenes of unmixed sorrow and saw two wretched souls tormented by a fiend, who without ceasing plunged them in liquid fire and burning brimstone while they at the same time accused and cursed each other. One of them said to his tormented fellow sufferer:

Cursed be your face that I ever set eyes on you! My misery is prolonged because of you. I have you to thank for this, for it was your influence that brought me here. You enticed me, and you ensnared me. It was your covetousness and cheating and your oppression and grinding of the poor that brought me here. If you had but set as good an example for me as you did an evil one, I might, for all I know, have been in heaven. There I would have been as happy as now I am miserable. O wretch that I was! My following your steps has put me in this contemptible state and ruined me forever. O that I had never seen your face or you had never been born to do my soul the wrong that you have done!

The other miserable person replied,

And may I not blame you as well? Do you not remember how at such a time and place you enticed me and drew me out? You asked me if I would go along with you when I was about other business, about my lawful calling. You lured me away; therefore, you are as much at fault as I. Though I was covetous, you were proud. And if you learned your covetousness from me, I am sure I learned my pride and drunkenness from you. Though you learned to cheat by watching me, you taught me to whore, to lie, and to scoff at goodness. Thus, though I caused you to stumble in some things, you tripped me up as much in others. Therefore, if you blame me, I can blame you as much. If I have to answer for some of your filthiest actions, you still have to answer for some of mine. I wish you had never come here. The very looks of you wound my soul by bringing sin afresh into my mind. It was with you that I sinned. O grief upon my soul! And since I could not shun your company there, O that I could have been without it here!

From this sad dialogue, I soon perceived that those who are companions on earth in sin will be so in hell in punishment. And though on earth they love each other's company, they will not care for it in hell. I believe this was the true reason why Dives, the rich man, seemed so charitable to his brothers. (See Luke 16:19–31.) He wanted them warned so that they might not come into the place of torment. It was love for himself and not for them that was his motive because had they come there, his torments would thereby have been increased.

A JUST PUNISHMENT

There were more tragic scenes of sorrow. Leaving those two cursed wretches accusing each other for being the authors of each other's misery, we passed on farther, observing several miserable spectacles. Among others, we saw one who had flaming sulfur forced down her throat by a tormenting spirit. He carried out this action with such horrid cruelty and insolence, I could not help but say to him:

Epenetus: Why should you so delight in tormenting that cursed wretch as to be perpetually pouring flaming and infernal liquid down her throat?

Fiend: This is no more than a just retribution. In her lifetime, this woman was such a sordid wretch that though she had enough gold, she could never be satisfied. Therefore, now I pour it down her throat. She did not care who she ruined and undid so that she could get their gold. When she had amassed a greater treasure than she could ever spend, her love of money would not let her spend so much of it as to supply herself with what the common necessities of life required. For then, she often went with an empty belly though her bags were full. Or else she satisfied her hunger at another's expense.

As for her apparel, it either never grew old, or if it did, it was always so supplied with patches that finally, it was as hard to say which piece was the original as it is among the learned men on earth to find out the origins of the Nile.

She kept no house because she would not be taxed. She did not keep her treasure in her hands, for fear she would be robbed, nor did she lease it for bonds and mortgages for fear of being cheated although she cheated all she could. She was so great a cheat that she robbed her body of its food and her own soul of mercy.

This cursed wretch had but one child in all the world to give her money to, but she had raised her so that the daughter knew no more how to make use of money than her mother did. Since gold then was her god on earth, is it not just that she should have her bellyful in hell?

When her tormentor had finished speaking, I asked her whether what he said were true or not. To this, she answered me, "No, to my grief, it is not."

"How to your grief?" said I.

She answered:

Because if what my tormentor tells you were true, I would be better satisfied. He tells you it is gold that he pours down my throat, but he is a lying devil and speaks falsely. If it were gold, I would never complain. But he abuses me, and instead of gold, he only gives me horrid, stinking sulfur. Had I my gold, I would still be happy. I value it so much that if I had it here, I scarcely would bribe heaven with it to be removed from here.

I could not help but tell my guide that I was amazed to hear a wretch in hell itself so idolize her riches even while she was in her tormentor's hands.

ABANDONED TO THE LOVE OF SIN

Angel: This may convince you that it is the love of gold that is the greatest of all evils. Where the love of gold prevails, that soul is lost forever. And therefore it is the greatest of all punishments to be abandoned to the love of sin. The love of gold to which this cursed creature is given up is a more exquisite and fatal punishment than what the apostate spirits here inflict on her.

Epenetus: Oh, could but wicked men on earth for one small moment place their ears at this mouth of Tophet (Isa. 30:33) and hear those horrid shrieks of damned souls, they could not be in love with sin again.

Angel: Eternal Truth has told us otherwise, for those who will not fear His ministers or have regard for what His Word contains will not be warned though one should come back from hell to warn them (Luke 16:31).

LIVING A DYING LIFE

We had not come much farther before we saw a wretched soul almost choked with brimstone lying on a bed of burning steel. He cried out as one suffering dreadful anguish. The note of desperation in his voice made me request my guide to stay awhile so that I might listen more attentively to what the tormented soul said. Then I heard him speak as follows:

Ah, miserable wretch! Undone forever, forever! O that killing word, *forever*! Not a million years will suffice to bear that pain, which, if I could avoid it, I would not bear one moment more for a million worlds! No, no, my misery will never have an end. After a million years, still it will be forever. O hapless, helpless, hopeless state indeed! Forever is the hell of hell! O cursed wretch! Cursed for all eternity! How willfully have I undone myself! What stupendous folly am I guilty of to choose sin's short and momentary pleasures at the costly rate of everlasting pain!

How often was I told it would be so! How often was I pressed to leave those paths of sin that would be sure to bring me to the chambers of eternal death! But I, like the deaf adder, lent no ear to those charmers, though they charmed so wisely. They told me often that my short-lived pleasures would quickly result in eternal pain. Now this too sad experience tells me it is so. It tells me so indeed, but it is too late to help it, for my eternal state is fixed forever.

Why did I have reason given to me? Why was I made with an immortal soul, and yet I took so little care of it? How my own neglect stings me to death, and yet I know I cannot, must not, die but live a dying life worse than ten thousand deaths. Yet I might once have helped all this, and I would not!

That is the gnawing worm that never dies. I might once have been happy. Salvation was offered to me, but I refused it. To refuse it once would have been a folly not to be forgiven, but it was offered to me a thousand times; yet, wretch that I was, I still as often refused it. O cursed sin, that with deluding pleasures bewitches mankind to eternal ruin! God often called, but just as often, I refused. He stretched His hand out, but I would not pay attention to it. How often have I ignored the wisdom of His counsel! How often have I refused His reproof!

But now the scene is changed; the case is altered. Now He laughs at my calamity and mocks that destruction that is come upon me. He would have helped me once, but then I would not; therefore, those eternal miseries I am condemned to undergo are but the just reward of my own doing.

I could not hear this doleful lamentation without reflecting on the wondrous grace the ever blessed God had showed to me. Eternal praises to His holy name! For my heart told me that I deserved to be the object of eternal wrath as much as that sad wretch, and it is His grace alone that has made us different.

O how unsearchable His counsels be!
And who can fathom His divine decree!

After these reflections, I addressed myself to the doleful complainer. I told him I had heard his woeful lamentation by which I perceived his misery was great and his loss irreparable. I said that I would willingly be informed of it more particularly, which might possibly be some alleviation of his sufferings.

Damned Soul: No, not at all. My pains are such as can admit no relief, no not for one small moment. But by the question you have asked, I perceive that you are a stranger here. May it ever be so. Had I but the least hope still remaining, how I would kneel and cry and pray forever to be redeemed from here, but all, it is all in vain. I am lost forever. But so that you may beware of coming here, I will tell you what the damned suffer.

WHAT THE DAMNED HAVE LOST

Damned Soul: Our miseries in this infernal dungeon are of two sorts: what we have lost and what we undergo. These I will reduce to their several parts although the sad recounting will give a greater sting to what I feel.

The Presence of God

Damned Soul: In this sad, dark abode of misery and sorrow, we have lost the presence of the ever blessed God; this is what makes this dungeon hell. If we had lost a thousand worlds, it would not be so much as this one loss. Could but the least glimpse of His favor enter here, we might be happy, but we have lost it to our everlasting sorrow.

Fellowship with the Saints and Angels

Damned Soul: Here we have likewise lost the company of the saints and angels. In their place, we have nothing but tormenting devils.

Heaven

Damned Soul: Here we have lost heaven, too, the seat of blessedness. There is a deep gulf between us and heaven, so that we are shut out from there forever. Those everlasting gates that permit the blessed into happiness are now forever shut against us here.

All Pity

Damned Soul: Here we have also lost all pity. To the miserable, this is a great loss. God so pities sinners that He has given His beloved Son to die for them, but to be so far from His pity that He rejoices in our misery and will do so forever is what stings us to the very heart. To lose God makes our misery miserable beyond measure. And what can be more cruel and tormenting than to have that Redeemer, who gave His very blood for others, refuse to pity us?

Nor will the saints and angels pity us; instead, while we here are howling in our misery under the wrath of an incensed God, the saints too will rejoice that we are damned, and God is glorified in our destruction. Behold the dismal consequence of our sin!

Hope and Help

Damned Soul: To make our wretchedness even more wretched, we have lost the hope of ever being in a better state, which renders our condition truly hopeless. He who on earth is the most miserable still has hope left as a reserve. Therefore, it is a common proverb there that were it not for hope, the heart would break. Well may our hearts break then since here we are without both hope and help.

WHAT THE DAMNED ENDURE

Damned Soul: This is what we have lost, which but to think on is enough to tear, rend, and gnaw on our miserable souls forever. O that this were all! But we have pain of sense as well as loss, and having showed you what we have lost, I am now going to show you what we undergo.

Unspeakable Torment

Damned Soul: First, we experience a variety of torments; we are tormented here a thousand, no, ten thousand separate ways. They who are most afflicted on earth have seldom any more than one disease at a time. But should they have the plague, the gout, the stone, and the fever, at one time, how miserable would they think themselves? Yet all these are but the biting of a flea to those intolerable, pungent pains that we endure. Here we have all the loathed variety of hell with which to grapple. Here is a fire that is unquenchable to burn us, a lake of burning brimstone ever choking us, eternal chains to tie us; here is utter darkness to frighten us, and a worm of conscience that gnaws on us everlastingly. Any one of these miseries is worse to bear than all the torments mankind ever felt on earth.

Simultaneous Torment

Damned Soul: But as our torments here are various, so are they universal too, afflicting each part of the body, tormenting all the powers of the soul, which makes what we suffer most unbearable. In those diseases men are seized with on earth, some parts are afflicted while other parts are not affected. Although your body may be out of order, your head may yet be well; though your head is ill, your vital organs may be free; or though your organs are affected, your arms and legs may still be clear. But here it is otherwise. Each member of the soul and body is tormented at once.

The eye is tormented with the sight of devils, who appear in all the horrid shapes and black appearances that sin can give them. The ear is continually tormented with loud yellings and continual outcries of the damned. The nostrils are smothered with sulfurous flames, the tongue with burning blisters, and the whole body rolled in flames of liquid fire.

All the powers and faculties of our souls are tormented here: the imagination, with thoughts of present pain; the memory, with reflecting on the heaven we have lost and those opportunities we had of being saved. Our minds are tormented with considering how vainly we have spent our precious time, and how we have abused it. Our understanding is tormented in the thoughts of our past pleasures, present pains, and future sorrows, which are to last forever, and our consciences are tormented with a continual gnawing worm.

Extreme Torment

Damned Soul: Another thing that makes our misery intolerable is the intensity of our torments. The fire that burns us is so violent that all the water in the sea could never quench it. The pains we suffer here are so extreme that it is impossible that they should be known by anyone but those who feel them. Godly justice here displays its power in the sustaining of our dying lives under those great and excruciating pains, which scarcely an angel's strength could endure.

Perpetual Torment

Damned Soul: Another of the sad ingredients of our misery is the continuity of our torments. As varied, as universal, and as extremely violent as they are, they are continual, too. Nor do we have the least intermission from them. Our miseries are both extreme and constant. If there were any relaxation, it might be some relief, but what makes our condition so deplorable is that there is no intermission in our torments. What we suffer now, we must suffer forever. This causes a hatred to rise in our hearts against God, and our hatred against God continues our miseries upon us.

Mutual Torment

Damned Soul: The society or company we have here is another ingredient in our misery. Tormenting devils and tormented souls are all our companions. Dreadful shrieks and howls caused by the fierceness of our pain and fearful blasphemy against Him whose power and justice keeps us here is all our conversation. And here the torments of our fellow sufferers are so far from relieving our misery that they increase our pain.

Place of Torment

Damned Soul: The location in which we suffer is another thing that increases our sufferings. It is the epitome of all misery: a prison, a dungeon, a bottomless pit, a lake of fire and brimstone, a furnace of fire that burns throughout eternity, the blackness of darkness forever, and lastly, hell itself. Such a wretched place as this must of necessity increase our wretchedness.

Cruel Tormentors

Damned Soul: The coldheartedness of our tormentors is another thing that adds to our anguish. Our tormentors are devils in whom there is no pity, but being tormented themselves, they take pleasure in tormenting us.

Everlasting Torment

Damned Soul: All those particulars that I have listed are very grievous, but what makes them much more intolerable is that they will ever be so. All our most unbearable sufferings will last throughout eternity. O wretched state of men to be the everlasting objects of God's revenging justice. To hear Him say, *"Depart from me, ye cursed, into everlasting fire"* (Matt. 25:41), is what perpetually sounds in my ears. O that I could reverse that fatal sentence! O that there was but a bare possibility of doing it! What is it that I would not do or suffer to cause it? And yet almighty power can inflict no more than what I suffer now. That I will suffer forever is what I do not know how to bear, yet what I must ever endure. Thus have I shown you the miserable case that we are in and will be in forever.

This wretched soul had scarcely made an end of what he was saying before he was tormented afresh by a hellish fury, who bid him cease complaining, for it was in vain. Addressing the damned, the tormentor said,

Do you not know you have deserved it all?
How often were you told of this before, but
you would not believe it then? You laughed at

136

them who told you of a hell.

No, you were so presumptuous to dare almighty Justice to destroy you. How often have you called on God to damn you? And do you now complain that you are answered according to your wishes? What an unreasonable thing is this that you should call so often for damnation and yet be so uneasy under it? You admit yourself that you had salvation offered to you, but you refused it. With what face then can you complain of being damned?

I have more reason to complain than you, for you have had many opportunities of repentance given to you, but I was condemned to hell as soon as I had sinned. You had salvation offered to you and pardon and forgiveness often extended to you, but I never had any mercy offered to me. I was consigned to everlasting punishment as soon as I had sinned. If I had had the offer of salvation, I never could have slighted it as you have done. It would have been better for you if you had never had the offer of it either, for then damnation would be easier for you to bear. Who do you think should pity you—you who would be damned in spite of heaven itself?

This made the wretch cry out,

O do not thus continue to torment me! I know that my destruction is my own fault. O that I could forget it! That thought is my greatest plague. I would be damned and, therefore, justly am so.

Then turning to the fiend that tortured him, he said,

But it was through your temptations, cursed devil, it was you that tempted me to all the sins I have been guilty of. Do you now upbraid me? You say you never had a Savior offered to you, but you should call to mind, you never had a Tempter either, as I have had continually of you, from whose unfortunate solicitations I never could be free.

To this the devil scornfully replied,

I admit it was my business to decoy you here, and you have often been told so by your preachers. They told you plainly enough that we sought your ruin. We went continually like roaring lions, seeking whom we could devour (1 Pet. 5:8). And I was often afraid you would believe them, as several did, to our great disappointment. But you were willing to do what we would have you, and since you have done our work, it is but reasonable that we should pay you your wages.

And then the fiend tormented him afresh, which caused him to roar out so horribly, I could no longer stay to hear him, and so I continued on.

Epenetus: How dismal is the condition of these damned souls. They are the Devil's slaves while on earth, and he upbraids and then torments them for it when they come to hell.

Angel: Their malice against all the race of Adam is exceedingly great because the blessed Redeemer died to save them, and they enjoy that happiness from which those spirits were cast down. And though it is impossible they should prevail on the elect so as to make one perish, since they know not who they are, they do not cease to tempt all to sin by all the means they can. Knowing that is the way to make them miserable and because many souls are ignorant of their devices, they easily prevail on them to their eternal ruin.

You have already seen, and will see more of it quickly, how they treat them here for listening to their temptations. And though they do it to satisfy the rage they have against them, they are therein the Almighty's agents and the just executioners of His deserved vengeance against sinners who will-fully destroy themselves by listening to the Devil.

GREATER TORMENT FOR FALSE WITNESSES

Passing a little farther, we saw a multitude of damned souls together, gnashing their teeth with extreme rage and pain, while the tormenting fiends with hellish fury poured liquid fire and brimstone continually on them. In the meantime, they cursed

God, themselves, and those about them, blaspheming after a fearful manner.

I could not help but ask of one fiend that so tormented them, who they were that he abused so cruelly.

Fiend: They are those who well deserve it. These are those cursed wretches who would teach others the right road to heaven while yet themselves were so in love with hell that they came here. These are those souls who have been the great agents of hell on the earth and therefore deserve a particular regard in hell. We use our utmost diligence to give everyone his share of torments, but we will be sure to take care that these will not lack for punishment. These have not only their own sins to answer for, but also all those of whom they have led astray, both by their doctrine and example.

Epenetus: Since they have been such great agents for hell as you say, I think gratitude should oblige you to treat them a little more kindly.

Fiend: If they expect gratitude among devils, they will find themselves mistaken. Gratitude is a virtue, but we hate all virtue and profess an immortal enmity against it. Besides, we hated all learning, and were it in our power, not one of them should be happy. It is true we do not tell them so on earth because there it is our business to flatter and deceive them, but when we have them here, when they are secure enough, for from hell there is no redemption, we soon convince them of their folly in believing us.

THE GREAT GRACE OF REDEMPTION

From the discourse I had heard from this and from other of the devils, I could not but reflect that it is infinite and unspeakable grace by which any poor sinners are brought to heaven, considering how many snares and baits are laid by the Enemy of souls to entrap them along the way.

Therefore, it is a work well worthy of the blessed Son of God to save His people from their sins and to deliver them from the *"wrath to come"* (1 Thess. 1:10). But it is an unaccountable madness and folly in men to refuse the offers of grace and to unite with the Destroyer.

Angel: It is sin that thus hardens their hearts and blinds their eyes so that they are incapable of making a right judgment of things until the Holy Spirit comes and anoints their eyes with His eye salve and makes the scales of ignorance and error drop off whereby they come to see things in a truer light. (See Acts 9:1–18.)

Going farther on, I heard a wretch complaining in a heartbreaking strain against those men who had betrayed him to this place.

TOO LATE FOR SALVATION

Damned Soul: I was told by those that I depended on and thought could have informed me right that if I only said, "Lord, have mercy on me" when I came to die, it would be enough to save me, but O how wretchedly I find myself mistaken to my eternal sorrow. Alas! I called for mercy on my deathbed but found it was too late. This cursed devil here that told me just before that I was safe enough then told me it was too late, and hell must be my portion as I find it is.

REAP WHAT YOU SOW

Devil: You see I told you true at last, and then you would not believe me. A very pretty business is it not, do you think? You spent your days in the pursuit of sin and wallowed in your filthiness and yet you thought you would go to heaven when you died. Would anyone but a madman think that that would ever do?

No, he who in good earnest intends to go to heaven when he dies must walk in the ways of holiness and virtue while he lives. You say some of your lewd companions told you that saying, "Lord, have mercy on me" when you came to die would be enough: a very fine excuse! You might have known if you would have given yourself enough leisure to have read the Bible that without holiness *"no one shall see the Lord"* (Heb. 12:14).

142

Therefore, this is the sum of the matter: you were willing to live in your sins as long as you could. You did not leave them at last because you did not like them, but because you could follow them no longer. You know this is the truth. And could you have the impudence to think to go to heaven with the love of sin in your heart? No, no such matter! You have been warned often enough that you should take heed of being deceived, for *"God is not mocked: for whatsoever a man soweth, that shall he also reap"* (Gal. 6:7); therefore, you have no reason to complain of anything but your own folly, which now you see too late.

Epenetus: This lecture of the devil was a very cutting one to the poor tormented wretch, and it contains the true case of many now on earth, as well as those in hell. But what a far different judgment do they make in this sad state from what they did on earth!

Angel: The reason is that while on earth, they will not allow themselves to think what the effects of sin will be or what an evil it is. Lack of attention is the ruin of thousands. They do not think about what they are doing or where they are going until it is too late to help it.

REGRET THAT COMES TOO LATE

We had not gone much farther before we heard another person tormenting himself and aggravating his own misery by reflecting on the happiness of blessed souls. He lamented:

> How brightly do the saints in heaven shine in the glory of the Divine Image while I am deformed! And yet I was once as capable of that glory as they. I had the same nature, the same reason, the same intellectual faculties and powers, but what a heinous monster I have now become that I should hate, and hate forever, the eternal Excellency. Now sin and death are finished with me. How vast is the difference between us! They have human nature in its most exalted beauty and perfection, but I, accursed I, have the same nature in its utmost depravity and corruption, which makes the comparison unspeakably far more unequal than that of the most amiable lovely person, flourishing in all the gaiety and prime of youthful strength and beauty to a putrefied and rotten carcass deformed by the corruption of a loathsome grave. All this amazing difference is a result of my willful and accursed sin! It is sin, it is only sin, that has undone me. As its just reward, sin has brought me here to suffer the dreadful vengeance of eternal fire.

ATHEISTS NO MORE

We were diverted from giving any further ear to the stinging self-reflections of this poor lost creature by seeing a vast number of tormenting fiends who were lashing incessantly with knotted whips of ever burning steel a numerous company of wretched souls while they roared out with cries so very piercing. They were all so lamentable that I thought it might have melted even cruelty itself into some pity. It made me say to one of the tormentors, "O stay your hand, and do not use such cruelty as this to these who are your fellow creatures and who perhaps you have yourselves betrayed to all this misery.

Devil: No, though we are bad enough, no devils ever were so bad as they, nor guilty of such crimes as they have been, for we all know there is a God, although we hate Him, but these are such as could never be brought to admit—until they came here—that there was such a Being.

Epenetus: Then these are atheists, a wretched sort of men indeed, who had once nearly ruined me if eternal grace had not prevented it.

I had no sooner spoken than one of the tormented wretches cried out with a mournful tone.

CONVERSATION WITH A FORMER ATHEIST

Damned Soul: I know that voice; it is Epenetus.

I was amazed to hear my name mentioned by one of the infernal crew; therefore, being desirous to know who it was, I answered.

Epenetus: Yes, I am Epenetus, but who are you in that sad, lost condition that knows me?

Damned Soul: I was once well acquainted with you on earth and had almost persuaded you to be of my opinion. I am the author of that celebrated book so well-known by the title of *Leviathan*.

Epenetus: What, *the* great Hobbes! Are you come here? Your voice is changed so much that I did not know it.

Hobbes: Alas! I am that unhappy man indeed. But I am so far from being great that I am one of the most wretched persons in all these soiled territories. Nor is it any wonder that my voice is changed, for I am now changed in my principles, though changed too late to do me any good. For now, I know there is a God, but I wish there were not, for I am sure He will have no mercy on me nor is there any reason that He should. I confess that I was His foe on earth, and now He is mine in hell where He makes me suffer all that almighty power can inflict or that a creature is able to sustain. To my eternal woe, I feel that I am now the subject of that power I once so wickedly derided. It is that wretched confidence I had in my own wisdom that has thus betrayed me.

Epenetus: Your case indeed is miserable, and yet you must admit that you suffer justly. For how industrious you were to make converts of others and so involve them in the same damnation! None has more reason to know this than I who almost was caught in the snare and perished irrecoverably.

Hobbes: To think how many perish by my means stings me to the heart. When I first heard your voice, I was afraid that you had likewise been consigned to punishment. Not that I can wish any person to be happy, for it is my plague to think that any are so while I am miserable, but because every soul that is brought here through my seduction while I was on earth doubles my pain in hell.

Epenetus: But tell me, for I would like to be informed, and you can do it, did you indeed believe, when on earth, there was no God? Could you imagine that the world could make itself and that the creatures were the causes of their own production? Had you no secret whispers in your soul that told you it was Another who made you, and not you yourself? (Ps. 100:3). And had you never any doubts about this matter?

I have often heard it said, when on earth, that though there are many who profess there is no God, there is not one who thinks so. It would be strange if there were because there is none who does not carry in his heart a witness for that God whom he denies. Now you can tell whether it is so or not, and you now have no reason to conceal your opinion.

Hobbes: Nor will I, Epenetus, although the thoughts sting me anew. At first, I did believe there was a God, who was that sovereign, self-subsistent Power, who gave life to all other creatures. But falling afterwards to vicious courses, which made me deserve His wrath, I had some secret wishes that there was none. It is impossible to think there is a God, and not, therefore, to think Him just and righteous, and, consequently, obliged to punish the transgressors of His law. Because I was aware that I deserved His justice, it made me hate Him and wish He did not exist. But still pursuing the same destructive courses and finding justice did not overtake me, I then began to hope there was no God.

From those hopes, I began to construct in my own mind ideas suitable to what I hoped. Having thus in my own thoughts framed a new system of the world's origin, excluding from it the existence of a Deity, I found myself so fond of those new notions that I at last prevailed on myself to give them credit. Then I endeavored to impose the belief of them on others. But before I came to such a height as this, I do acknowledge that I found several checks in my own conscience for what I did.

All along, I would now and then be troubled with some strange, uneasy thoughts as if I should not find all right at last, but I endeavored to put them off as much as I could. And now I find those checking thoughts that might have been of service to me then are here the things that torment me most of all.

And I must admit, the love of sin hardened my heart against my Maker and made me hate Him first and then deny His existence. Sin, that I hugged so close to my heart, has been the cursed cause of all this woe. The Serpent has stung my soul to death. For now I find, in spite of my vain philosophy and those new systems I endeavored to impose on the world, there is a God, and He is a *"great and terrible"* (Neh. 1:5) one.

I also find that God will not be mocked (Gal. 6:7). It was my daily practice in the world to mock heaven and ridicule whatever things were sacred, which were the means I used to spread abroad my cursed notions. I always found these methods very successful, for those I could get to ridicule the Sacred Oracles, I always looked on favorably to become my disciples. But now the thoughts thereof are more tormenting to me than all the torments I sustain by whips of burning steel. For nothing more provokes the offended Majesty of heaven than to ridicule what He has made so worthy.

Epenetus: By what you have said, it is easy to discern the great malignity of sin against the ever blessed God from whose most righteous will and law it is a deviation. And it was alone your giving way to sin that imposed all your miseries on you. And, doubtless, it is a cruel and tormenting thought to think that what you suffer is most just. But it is not my design to aggravate your miseries, only I would ask another question that I would be resolved in. I heard you and others in the same condition with you, cry out because of burning steel and fire and flame, and yet I cannot discern it. Where there is fire, there must be some degree of light, and yet it appears to me, you are still in complete darkness.

Hobbes: O if only I could say I felt no fire, how easy my torments would be to what I now find them. But alas! The fire that we endure ten thousand times exceeds all culinary fire in fierceness and is of a quite different nature from it, which you already well observed in one particular, which is, that there is no light at all that attends it as does the fire that burns on earth. Notwithstanding all the fire in hell, we are in utter darkness.

But then the fire you burn on earth is of a preying and devouring nature, for whatever it takes hold of, it consumes to ashes. When it meets with no more fuel, it goes out. But here it is not so, for though it burns with a tremendous fierceness, which none but those who feel it know, it does not consume, nor never will. We will ever be burning, yet not burned. It is a tormenting but not consuming fire.

The fire that is burned on earth is a physical fire and cannot seize on immaterial substances, and such are souls. But here, the fire seizes our souls and puts them into pain so exquisite and so tormenting as cannot be expressed. It was my ignorance of this that when on earth made me ridicule the notion of immaterial substances being burnt by fire, which here to my own cost I find too true.

And then another difference from the fire that burns on earth is this: you can kindle earthly fire whenever you please and quench it when you will, but here it is otherwise. This fire is kindled by the breath of heaven, like a stream of brimstone, and it burns forever. Therefore, it is most properly described as *"fire unquenchable"* (Luke 3:17), which here is likely to be our everlasting portion. And this is my answer to the last sad question that you asked me.

Epenetus: Sad indeed! See what Almighty Power can inflict on those who violate His righteous law.

I was making some further observations on what I heard when the relentless fiend, who before was tormenting them, interrupted me.

Devil: You see by him what sort of men they were when in the world. Do you not think that they deserve the punishment they undergo?

Epenetus: Doubtless it is the just reward of sin, which now they suffer and which hereafter you will suffer too. For you, as well as they, have sinned against the ever blessed God, and for your sin, you will suffer the just vengeance of eternal fire. Nor is it in the least any excuse to say that you never doubted the existence of God. For though you knew there was a God, you rebelled against Him. Therefore, you may be justly punished with everlasting destruction from the presence of the Lord and from the glory of His power.

Devil: It is true we know we will be punished as you have said. But if it is a reason why mankind should have pity shown to them because they fell for the temptations of the Devil, it is the same case with me and all the rest of the inferior spirits. We were tempted by the bright Sun of the Morning to take part with him. Therefore, though this aggravates the crime of Lucifer, it should lessen the blame for inferior spirits.

To this my bright guide who had not spoken to them since my coming here thus replied, with a stern, angry countenance,

Angel: O you apostate, wicked, lying spirit! Can you affirm those things and see me here? Do you not know that it was your proud heart that made you take part with Lucifer against the blessed God, who had created you a glorious creature! But priding yourself in your own beauty, you desired to be above your blessed Creator. You were ready to take part with Lucifer and justly are cast down to hell with him. Your former comeliness and beauty are changed to that horrid, monstrous form in which now you appear. It is the just punishment of your rebellious pride.

Devil: Why do you thus invade our territories and come here to torment us before our time? (See Matthew 8:28–29.)

When the devil had said this, he slunk away as if he did not dare to stay to hear the answer.

The fiend being gone, I said to my guide that I had already heard about the fall of the apostate angels, but that I had a great desire to be informed in the particulars thereof more fully.

Angel: Once you have put off your mortality and are translated to the blessed above, there you will know such things as now you cannot apprehend. Therefore, in your present state, do not desire to be wise above what is written. It is enough to know the angels sinned, and for their sin, they were cast down to hell. But how pure spirits should have a thought rise in their hearts against the Eternal Purity that first created them is what you are not capable of comprehending now.

The angelic spirits are free agents, all created so by the Almighty, who loves to have a free and willing service offered to Him by all His creatures. And this, the Sacred Oracles inform you, is called a reasonable service (Rom. 12:1). Angels had a time for their probation, even in heaven, as well as Adam had in Paradise. Like him, they were created with the possibility of falling, but as the fall of Adam was repaired by the great promise of the blessed Messiah, so all those blessed spirits who kept their stations in the great defection of the apostate angels, are, through the wondrous grace of the Messiah, confirmed. Forever, He is the Head of angels, too, as well as men. In all things, He has the preeminence (Col. 1:18), for He is the eternal Son of God.

But you have seen enough in these black realms of misery and woe to show the glory of eternal justice, which even the damned spirits acknowledge to be so. For when that great Deciding Day will come, when the bodies of the dead will rise and be united to their souls again and then appear before the judgment seat, there is none of these black souls who will not plead guilty and justify the judgment of damnation that they will then hear God pronounce against them.

Epenetus: I have observed that all of them complain most of the torment that arises from their own sense of guilt, which justifies the justice of the punishment. This gloomy prison is the best mirror in which to behold sin in its most proper colors. For if there were not the greatest malignity in sin, it would not be rewarded with so extreme a punishment.

Angel: Your inference is very natural, but there is a better mirror than this to see the just demerits due to sin: by contemplating the blessed Son of God on the cross. There we may see the dire effects of sin; there we may see its true malignity. For all the sufferings of the damned here are but the sufferings of creatures still, but on the cross, you see a suffering God.

Epenetus: Surely, justice and mercy never so triumphed and kissed each other (Ps. 85:10) as in that fatal hour. For justice there was fully satisfied in the just punishment of sin, and mercy triumphed and was pleased because hereby salvation for poor sinners was effected. And O, eternal praises to His holy name forever that by His grace, He has made me willing to accept this salvation, and thereby to become an heir of glory. For I remember some of those lost wretches who have, in their bitter lamentations, urged that when salvation was offered to them, they refused it. It was, therefore, grace alone that helped me to accept it.

My shining guardian told me then that he must now conduct me to the earth again and leave me there to wait with faith and patience until my expected happy change should come. He added that it would be my wisdom to retain always a due sense of my own unworthiness, for to be vile in my own eyes would make me precious in the sight of God. I should not take that caution ill because the Enemy of souls is filled with temptations to puff up those who have had great discoveries and revelations of the mind of God, for there is nothing that the Devil aims at more than to destroy those who are most dear to God. Though he ever fails in his attempts, he is unwearied still in his endeavors; oftentimes, he prevails so far against them as to persuade them to commit those sins, which makes them afterwards go mourning to their graves.

I thanked my guide for the good counsel he had given me and told him I would be lacking in gratitude if I did not accept it as the greatest kindness he could show me.

Angel: Come then, and let us leave these realms of woe and horror to the possession of their black inhabitants.

And in a very little space of time, I found myself on earth again. I was back in that very place where I planned to have committed that black sin of being my own murderer, overcome by the temptations of the Devil, who had persuaded me that there was no God, as I related in the beginning of this book. But what way it was that I came there I am not at all able to determine. As soon as I was by the bank that I had sat on before, the bright appearance by whom I had been guided all along said to me:

Angel: Now Epenetus, you know where you are, and I must stay no longer with you now. I have another ministry to attend. Praise Him who sits upon the throne forever, who has all power in heaven, earth, and hell:

For all the wonders of His love and grace,
Which He has shown you in so short a space.

RETURNED HOME

As I was going to reply to him, my bright guide disappeared, and I was left alone. Having for some time considered the amazing visions I had seen and the wondrous things that I had heard, I scarcely believed I was on earth again. Nor did I know how long I had been absent. Resolving to return to my own home, I first knelt down and prayed that I might never lose a keen sense of all those wondrous things that had been shown to me. Then, I rose again, blessing and praising God for all His goodness and much admiring His wondrous grace and condescension.

A VISIBLE CHANGE

As I returned to my house, my family was very surprised to see my countenance so strangely changed. They looked at me as if they had scarcely known me.

I asked them the meaning of their unusual admiration.

They answered that it was the change in my appearance that had caused it.

I asked them in what respect I was altered.

They told me that yesterday my looks were so extremely clouded and cast down I seemed to be the very image of despair. But now, my face appeared abundantly more beautiful and reflected all the marks of perfect joy and satisfaction in it.

I told them that if they had seen what I had seen today, they would not wonder at the changes they saw. Then going into my room, I took my pen and ink and there wrote down what I had heard and seen, declaring all of the visions from the first to the last. I hope that all of my words may have the same effect on those who read them as they have had on me in writing them. *"Now unto the King eternal, immortal, invisible, the only wise God, be honour and glory for ever and ever. Amen"* (1 Tim. 1:17).